The Witch of Lagg

Ann Pilling

Collins

An imprint of HarperCollins*Publishers*

First published in Armada by Collins 1985
This edition 2000

Collins is an imprint of HarperCollins*Publishers* Ltd
77–85 Fulham Palace Road, Hammersmith,
London, W6 8JB

The HarperCollins website address is:
www.fireandwater.com

1 3 5 7 9 8 6 4 2

Text copyright © Ann Cheetham 1985
ISBN 0 00 710269 0

The author asserts the moral right to be
identified as the author of the work.

Printed and bound in Great Britain by
Omnia Books Limited, Glasgow

CHAPTER ONE

"My back's killing me," Colin grumbled, trying to get the rickety wheelbarrow back on to the path again, "and this barrow's falling to pieces. Can't Mr Grierson get you a new one? How can he expect you to manage with a thing like this?"

Duncan Ross shrugged, and his brown freckled face darkened slightly. It always did when anyone mentioned Hugo Grierson of Lagg Castle. He was a great landowner, one of the wealthiest men in this part of Scotland, and one of the meanest, according to Duncan's father Angus, who worked for him.

"Och, A've tel't ye already," the boy said, "he's awfu' tight wi' money. He'd like fine to have us awa' from here. Have ye no' seen our hoos?"

They certainly had. Ramshaws was a crumbling stone hut high in the trees above Carlin's Crag, the great white rock face that gashed this dark green woodland like a huge hunk of bone. The Ross's cottage had walls that ran with damp, no electricity, and rotting window frames.

Colin wanted to climb the Crag but it was highly dangerous, and all fenced off with barbed wire. The views from up there must be fabulous, with the dark green pine forests spreading down to the sea, and a glimpse across to the English Lake District on a clear day. Lagg Castle, where he was staying for the summer with his sister Prill and their cousin Oliver, was just inland from the coast, overlooking the Solway Firth. They were only fifty miles across the English border, here in the Scottish Lowlands, but it felt like another world.

Today they were too deep in the woods for any kind of view, helping Duncan to dismantle a huge pile of stones in the garden of an empty cottage called Lochashiel. The stones were needed to repair a wall that had collapsed in one of Hugo Grierson's fields, and the three children had been sent out to give Duncan a hand. The stones were so heavy, and the children had had to make so many journeys with them, that the ancient barrow really did look as if it was ready to fall apart.

"It's pretty here," Prill said, looking across the tangled garden at the small white-washed cottage. "Why doesn't he let you live in this? You'd only need to tidy up a bit, and give it a lick of paint – and it's much nearer the road. You wouldn't have that awful long track to climb, if you lived here."

"Aye," muttered Duncan, looking even gloomier. "That's true. But he wants to make money out of the place. Ma faither was born in this hoos, and it's ours, by rights, but Grierson says he's keepin' it for holiday folk."

"But there's nobody in it," Oliver pointed out. "The

furniture's all covered with dust sheets. I've looked."

"You *would*," Colin said irritably. "Why don't you give us a hand with this lot, instead of snooping about, peeping through windows? Some holiday this is going to be. Honestly, I've had just about enough!" He sat down grumpily in the middle of the mossy forest path, abandoning the wheelbarrow and its load.

"Let's have something to eat," Prill suggested, trying to be tactful. She knew Colin was spoiling for a fight with Oliver. "There are some buns in this bag, and a bottle of lemonade."

"Home-made," Oliver said proudly.

Colin would have preferred Coke to the sour, gritty concoction provided by Oliver's mother, his Great Aunt Phyllis, but she said fizzy drinks rotted your teeth and kept you awake at night. Everything was going to be home-made for the next few weeks because she was in charge of all the cooking.

Lochashiel was on the lower fringes of a vast plantation, which belonged to Hugo Grierson. David Blakeman, Colin and Prill's father, had come up to Scotland to paint the master of Lagg. He was an art teacher at a big comprehensive school but he sometimes got commissions for portraits. Not enough to give up teaching, though, which was what he really wanted to do.

His wife had stayed behind to look after Grandma

Blakeman. She'd just recovered from very bad influenza and the doctor said she shouldn't really be left. She'd actually caught it from Mrs Blakeman, and neither of them were feeling too fit. "It's a case of one old crock looking after another," their mother had laughed, pale-faced but cheerful, waving them off a few days before. Dad had been keen to do this Scottish portrait but when his wife fell ill, and Mr Grierson phoned to say his housekeeper had just given in her notice and left, he thought the whole plan would have to be scrapped. The children couldn't run round the place unsupervised, the man had made that *quite* clear. Then Great Aunt Phyllis came to the rescue.

She was Grandma's younger sister and Oliver was her adopted son. They lived with miserable Uncle Stanley in a London flat at the top of 9, Thames Terrace, a forlorn-looking house near the river where she looked after six elderly people and where Oliver had to creep round in soft shoes, and whisper all the time, in case he annoyed the old folk.

They'd all gone away for the summer, while repairs were being done to the house, but Uncle Stanley had refused to budge. He didn't trust those workmen, they might steal his books, or interfere with his collections.

Aunt Phyllis was all for getting Oliver out of London, away to the country, and when Dad told her that the holiday was off because Hugo Grierson had just lost his housekeeper she immediately offered to help.

Mum could stay behind with Grandma, and get her strength up again, and she would cope with the family, Oliver, his two older cousins, and their little sister Alison who was just walking. The toddler had her moments but she was no match for her Aunt Phyllis. After years of handling difficult old people, and years before that as a hospital matron, she reckoned she could manage Alison blindfold, with one hand tied behind her back."

Rather to Dad's surprise, Mr Grierson had agreed instantly, over the phone. His main concern was to have peace and quiet for the painting sessions, and not to be disturbed by a troop of noisy children. Aunt Phyllis sounded ideal.

"It's all worked out beautifully," she'd announced, patting her new steel-grey perm when they eventually met up at Dumfries Station, but one look at Oliver and the Blakemans' spirits sank. He'd muscled in on their family holiday yet again, and this time all his pernickety, nit-picking habits would be reinforced by his mother.

Anyway, if either of them upset Alison it was going to be all-out war. They'd agreed that on the train.

"She's not going to be bossed round by those two," Prill had said fiercely. "She's only little, and they'll just have to make allowances. Aunt Phyllis is always so mad keen to get people *organized*. Ugh!"

It was their aunt who'd roped them in for this rock-shifting exercise. She firmly believed that "the devil made work for idle hands to do" and when she'd discovered that Duncan was expected to do the job all on his own she'd immediately dispatched the children up to Lochashiel.

"Go and give the poor boy a bit of help," she'd ordered, immediately after breakfast. "Get some fresh air in those lungs. Four pairs of hands are better than one. Lunch at twelve-thirty sharp. I'll cope with Alison."

Oliver hadn't wanted to touch those stones at all. The first couple of days with his cousins were always difficult anyway, because he irritated Colin, who made no secret of the fact, but the minute he saw the huge heap, piled up like a cairn on the top of a mountain, in the middle of that cottage garden, he knew that there was something special about it, and that it shouldn't be tampered with.

He'd said nothing, realizing they'd probably laugh at him, or say he'd got a bee in his bonnet, as usual. Instead, he'd hung about by the little garden gate as the other three inspected the mysterious rocky mound, with cold shivers running up and down his back, silently willing them to leave the thing alone. When they started to load the barrow he came forward very reluctantly, but he didn't offer to help. Prill and Colin knew he wasn't strong, and he was ill quite a lot. He'd trade on that if the Scots boy tried to get him working.

He stood watching nervously while the others removed the first few layers of stones and chucked them into the barrow. When two loads had been wheeled down to the field, and they were doing a third, Oliver peered forward and suddenly put a hand on the greenish mossy stones that were now coming to light. They were damp.

"I bet it's a well," he said quietly, a strange excitement creeping into his voice. He jabbed at the boulders with a stick. "Look, you can see now. It's definitely circular, and these stones have sunk in a bit. I bet that's what it is."

Duncan glanced across at Oliver as he took a swig from the lemonade bottle. This boy puzzled him. A queer staring look had come into his eyes when he saw the cairn, his thin little body had gone all rigid for a minute and he had obviously been very reluctant to join in. The Scots boy wasn't too impressed. It was a hard job they were doing, and he needed all the help he could get. The girl hadn't been able to do very much, because most of the stones were just too heavy for her to lift, but this boy could have surely had a go. His first attempt had sent him staggering backwards and his second had grazed his knuckles. He'd then spent a full five minutes complaining, and inspecting his injuries, and after that he'd not helped at all; instead he'd fiddled round by the well, poking round with a penknife and putting bits of rubbish in his pockets. He just didn't like hard work. Oliver didn't exactly resemble Superman. He was thin and bony, and short for his age, and he wore thick black glasses that gave him an owlish look.

"I reckon it'll take maybe another twa loads to finish this job," Duncan grunted, casting a scowl at Oliver as he helped Colin back on to the track with the barrow. "Aye, an' yon laddie's neither use nor ornament the noo."

"No," Colin muttered in embarrassment. "It's a bit typical I'm afraid. He's a skiver. I'd like to tell him exactly what I think of him but it's rather difficult with his mother always breathing down our necks."

He could have said a lot more about his cousin but he decided to keep quiet. They'd been on holiday together before and Oliver got weird ideas about all sorts of things. Events had often proved him right, but somehow Colin didn't want to embark on all that, not with this straightforward Scots boy. He'd certainly noticed Oliver's odd reaction to the cairn of stones, his bulging eyes, his shaking; he might tackle him about it later, when they were on their own. He knew his cousin wouldn't say anything himself, he was too secretive.

They were tireder than they knew after all the fetching and carrying. Colin could hardly push the barrow along the path, though it was downhill all the way to the field.

"Is it stuck?" said Prill, tugging at the rough wooden handles. "Let's all pull together. One, two, *three*... there you are. You're off." And Colin staggered away into the trees with his creaking load.

He was halfway down the track when something

odd happened. At first he thought it was that idiot Oliver playing tricks on him. He was pushing his barrow along, quite enjoying the smell of the pine needles, and the stillness of the deep woods, when someone suddenly jumped on to his back.

"*Hey!*" he shouted, dropping the handles, "What on *earth*..." It was the kind of thing Alison did sometimes. She'd get up on to a stool or table, leap on his shoulders and beg for a piggy-back ride. Cold little fingers were clutching at his neck *now*, and there was a funny whistling noise in his ears. He spun round, but the weight on his back made him lurch about and he fell sprawling into the bracken. The barrow tipped over and its load went crashing on to the path. One of the biggest stones hit Colin's foot, right on the instep where there was hardly any flesh. It was terribly painful, even through his sneakers.

"*Ouch!*" he yelled, hopping about, and rubbing. But someone was actually laughing at him, a thin, high-pitched laugh that seemed to set the nearest bushes rustling. A spiteful kind of cackle that sent cold shivers through him.

His foot was so painful that he felt quite sick. He sat down, closed his eyes, and dropped his head down between his knees. When he looked up again Duncan was peering down at him anxiously. He had two massive boulders, one under each arm, and he was sweating.

"What's come ower ye, man?" he asked.

"I... I..." Colin began feebly, but words failed him. There was nobody else on the path at all, and the other two were still up at Lochashiel. Yet it *had* to be Oliver who'd pounced on him like that. Who else could it have been?

"What's wrang wi' ye?" repeated Duncan, looking at him curiously, then at the overturned barrow, and the litter of stones.

"Someone jumped out at me," Colin said, still rubbing his foot, "and they must have run off into the woods. I – heard them laughing." He got to his feet again, but he swayed slightly. The weight didn't seem to have gone away somehow. He must have ricked his back, humping all those stones about.

"Sit you doon, man," ordered Duncan. "Ye look like ye've seen a wee ghaist. I'll put the stanes back; you bide where y'are a wee while."

Colin watched him reload the barrow. He puffed and sweated as if each stone weighed a ton. It was as if they'd doubled in size on their way down from Lochashiel, and he kept dropping them. It was the slimy ones from the bottom, presumably, that would keep slipping through his fingers.

He'd only just finished when Prill and Oliver came out of the trees. The skinny young boy was carefully cleaning the blades of his penknife but Prill was looking into the woods. She kept turning her head from side to side, and sniffing.

"I'm right you know, Oll. Someone *has* been along here. You should tell your father, Duncan. Mr Grierson's got intruders."

"What? Here in the wood? That'll be holiday folk from yon tents in the long field." He shrugged. "Ye canna do ower much aboot that. It's no' agin the law to trespass here in Scotland, unless harm's done."

"But they *have*," said Prill. "They've been lighting fires. Can't you smell anything?"

Duncan sniffed. Someone had certainly been burning something, and close at hand. It was a warm day with no wind, yet you could smell smoke drifting over from somewhere.

"It's like this all along the path," Prill went on, "Right back to Lochashiel. It looks as if someone's been along here with a blow-lamp, or something. Look at the ground."

Underfoot the moss was ashy, turned to black velvet then all broken up into crumbly pieces by their feet. On both sides of the track the low bushes were brown and scorched, their leaves hanging off them limply, like dirty twisted ribbons.

Duncan pulled a face. "I must tell ma faither aboot this. If his plantations take light I don't doubt yon Grierson'll have a fit, then we'll be oot in a crack. Looks like there's some daftie hereabouts. Colin heard snickerin' when he tripped wi' yon stanes."

"*How* did you trip?" said Oliver suspiciously,

examining the path. "It's quite smooth here. I can't understand it."

"Those stones are heavy," Colin replied, quite savagely. "You'd know, if you'd actually bothered to help. It... I just fell sideways, and the whole lot went flying."

"But I still can't—"

"Oh shut *up*, Oll," Prill said anxiously. She didn't like the look of Colin at all. He kept rubbing at his back and his neck, his face was very white, and he was shivering. She hoped the dreaded flu bug hadn't followed them up to Scotland.

She felt cold herself as they all helped push the last barrow-load down to the field. But the cold didn't seem to come from the woods. It was uncanny. It was at their backs, all the way along the blackened track, yet it was a warm day and the trees were dangerously dry, according to Duncan. The path was so withered and burnt it was hard to believe that anything green would ever grow here again.

Oliver looked at the scorched bushes in uneasy silence and when he thought of that great stone cairn he felt frightened. They'd disturbed something today, something very ancient and perhaps sacred, something no one had meddled with for years and years. He didn't like this uncanny icy feeling in the middle of the sun-dappled woodland, and he didn't like Colin's accident, or the sound of that crazy laughter either.

What had they done? What had they started? Oliver had the distinct feeling that this episode in the forest was only the beginning.

CHAPTER TWO

"I feel like the Salvation Army," said Colin. "All I need's my trombone."

They were walking slowly down the long dark drive of Lagg Castle, away from the house. He was carrying a pan of hot soup and Oliver held a complete dinner covered up with a plate. Prill had their red setter Jessie on a lead in one hand, the other grasped her little sister's arm firmly. There was quite a fast road at the bottom of the drive. It'd be just like Jessie to see a rabbit and bolt across after it, and Alison might run straight after her.

"Look to the right, look to the left, and over we go," chanted Oliver, leading the party with his meat and two veg. Colin and Prill grinned at one another slyly. He was just like his mother. Now they knew where all those irritating little quotes of his came from.

They were taking some dinner to Granny MacCann. "It's your good deed for the day," Aunt Phyllis told them. "She's been rather poorly."

"Thought we'd done our good deed," Colin had whispered to Prill as the dinner was arranged on its plate. "What was this morning's caper? A picnic or something? And when's she going to let us off the hook? I want to explore. Duncan says there's a marvellous beach nearby, and there's a castle somewhere, on a little island."

"Well, it gets us out of washing up."

"Yes, but she's roped Dad in to do that, then Mr Grierson'll be ringing his bell and he'll have to go running back up to the studio. It's like training for the Army."

The spindly legs of their young cousin had already disappeared up the woodland path, though they could see the dinner plate, flashing in and out of the trees. The main road cut through the Forest of Lagg. The woods went on for miles on this side. Granny MacCann lived half a mile along the lower track quite near Lochashiel, in a cottage with a small field sloping up to it from the road, where sheep grazed and the afternoon sun dappled the trees above. From here Carlin's Crag was a terrifying overhang. The strong light made it gleam smooth and white like an enormous polished skull. The tiny cottage below was tucked in, under its shadow, and there were stones on the roof, Colin noticed. Bad weather must have brought those down from the Crag. What a place for an eighty-year-old woman to live, all alone.

Granny MacCann had been cook and housekeeper at Lagg for years, and she'd gone on doing it into her seventies. Nobody had been satisfactory since she'd left, according to Grierson. People never stayed longer than a month or two. The children hadn't met Hugo Grierson yet but they didn't much like what they'd heard about him. He was obviously very mean with the Rosses and they resented his attitude to their father too. He'd had an electric bell rigged up in the basement and Mr Blakeman was supposed to go running up to his rooms the minute it rang. Mr Grierson seemed to think he could buy people, body and soul, and do just what he liked with them.

Granny MacCann was one of the few people around that Grierson didn't interfere with. She'd rocked him in his cradle up in the old nursery at Lagg, and there was nothing she didn't know about him. He never went to visit her but he did keep her in firewood, and the Rosses were sent down to check on her when the weather was bad. Occasionally he even had the odd repair done to her cottage and Hugo Grierson rarely spent money on anything, unless, like this portrait, it added to his own grand image of himself.

Granny MacCann was enthroned in a big carver chair by a small fire. There was nothing faint or feeble about the strong Scots voice that bade them, "Come along in wi' ye," when they knocked. In fact something in the harsh tone of command was a bit frightening, and when Oliver pushed the door open, and they all crept inside, they were frankly terrified.

Aunt Phyllis thought she was eighty plus, but she was surely into her nineties. Her long pendulous nose drooped down, her sharp old woman's chin curved up to meet it, and in between was a black hole of a mouth displaying three yellow teeth. She was looking at them curiously, with eyes of the oddest whitish-green colour; little eyes they were, like chips of pale stone in her worn mahogany face, eyes that missed nothing.

The old woman had hardly any hair. What was left strayed out from under a little knitted cap and, in spite of the fire, she sat swathed in layers of woolly shawls. She wore grey mittens and her fingernails, greeny-white like her eyes, had grown so long they curved right over, like something in a horror comic. If it hadn't been for the television in one corner, and the fact that her stout little legs were encased in trendy striped warmers, Oliver really would have said she was a witch.

Colin and Prill were thinking of witches too, Colin of his grandmother's Arthur Rackham fairy book which he'd always had to read with very clean hands, and Prill about Hansel and Gretel and the witch roasting children in her oven. She wanted to give the old woman her dinner and make a quick exit. The pretty cottage, approached across a burn through a small grove of rowan trees, was much less appealing inside, and as for Granny MacCann herself...

"Come to your grannie then," the old woman whispered to Alison, and to everyone's amazement the little girl toddled across the filthy floor, climbed up into the woolly lap, and buried herself in the shawls. Prill was staggered. Alison was rather a difficult child and very

23

particular about her likes and dislikes. She disliked quite a few people, and getting her to stay anywhere for longer than five minutes was a real pain. Granny MacCann was talking some unintelligible Scottish gibberish to her, through great mouthfuls of food, and Alison was listening, and stroking a large cat.

It was a moth-eaten, black and white tom, an ugly creature with only one ear and a vicious look in its greenest of green eyes. The old woman introduced it affectionately as "ma wee Dandy". It spat at Jessie, and arched its back, but instead of going for it, the big dog cowered away whining, rubbing herself against Prill's legs. Jessie was six times as big as Dandy, but she seemed frightened of him.

The old woman knew all about their stone-moving, up at Lochashiel, and she obviously didn't approve. "Ye'll stir things up, laddie," she said, wagging one filthy finger at Oliver who'd crept up close, for a better view. "Young Aggie Ross'll be oot after ye, that she will…"

Oliver started when he heard that, and a sudden wave of cold swept over him. "Who's Aggie Ross?" he said, in a hoarse whisper.

The cottage was smelly, and Prill had backed away to stand near the open door. She was looking out into the garden, longing to get away, but Colin was standing near Oliver, and saw everything. When his cousin nearly jumped out of his skin at the name of Aggie Ross their eyes met, just for a moment, and in that moment they both saw the same thing, the barrow going over, and the huge heap of stones, and they heard the spiteful laughter echoing through the woods.

"*Aggie Ross,*" Oliver repeated, touching the old woman's skirt. "Who is she?"

If Granny MacCann had heard she pretended not to. She crooned over Alison and stroked the mangy old cat and pressed her shrivelled lips together very firmly. But Oliver, staring very hard at her, in that maddening way of his, saw fear in the ancient face, and perhaps a regret that she'd ever mentioned Aggie Ross.

It felt different in the cottage now, the fire had guttered to a single flame and the old Scots lullaby had stopped abruptly. Outside the sun had gone behind a cloud and the low room was suddenly dark and wintry. "*She'll be oot after ye...*" What could it mean?

As usual Oliver's busy brain was racing ahead but he *must* go one step at a time. Aggie Ross could well be some distant relative of Angus and Duncan; on the other hand she may be just a local busybody, someone who occasionally rented Lochashiel and didn't want a troop of kids messing up her garden. They'd have to ask Duncan next time they saw him. After Granny MacCann the Rosses knew more about Lagg Castle and its estate than anyone else around, even though they'd lived in England for a year or so. They'd come back after old Mrs Grierson had died. She'd promised Lochashiel to them, on her death bed, but there was no will. So everything had gone to her son Hugo. Angus Ross hated him for that.

As for moving that heap of stones, Duncan had made nothing of it. So if there *was* a sinister story attached to the cairn he obviously didn't know a thing about it. His father might know though.

Prill was signalling wildly for the boys to grab Alison and say goodbye, but Oliver wouldn't budge. He was fascinated by the cottage. The smell and the filth didn't bother him at all, he was used to very old people. They hoarded all kinds of rubbish in their bedsitters at home, and old rags and bones were bound to smell a bit if you couldn't get in to clean properly. There *were* bones too, all along the window ledges and on the mantelpiece, the skulls of badgers and sheep and mice, the rib cages of birds and what looked like the backbone of a deer. For the old woman to have bones littered round the place struck him as distinctly peculiar until he remembered that Granny MacCann had got seven children and fifteen grandchildren. At various ages they must have often wandered in to this cottage with their treasures from the woods. These were the remains.

Over the fireplace some tiny bones were fanned round in the shape of a star and underneath there were strings and strings of withered red berries. The old woman wore a similar string round her neck. "Tis to keep the de'il awa frae the hoos, laddie," she croaked, as he fingered the dusty necklaces that hung from the mantelpiece. "Plant rowans and the de'il'll no' come near ye."

Prill and Colin went outside, muttering their goodbyes, followed by a grizzling Alison who would have obviously stayed with the old woman all day. Prill couldn't understand it. Granny MacCann's was a face she would dream about in nightmares.

As they waited for Oliver, a fat, untidy-looking woman with a baby in her arms pushed past them, into the house. "And how are ye today, Grann?" she said, in a loud harsh voice. She paid no attention whatever to the three children. Perhaps, in these parts, you were always avoided if you were known to be guests of Hugo Grierson.

They were trailing back along the track towards the road when an awful noise behind made them all whip round. It sounded as if a mad dog had been let loose in a home for stray cats. There was a screaming and a spitting, and a series of ear-splitting howls, and they saw Dandy in the cottage garden, his fur all prickly like a black and white porcupine, tearing up and down the patch of grass, then round in mad circles, faster and faster, chasing his own tail, then racing up a tall birch by the gate, absolutely vertical, like something shot from a gun. They couldn't see the cat now but they could hear it only too well. It was howling and screeching wildly, shaking all the branches as if every devil in hell was after it.

"What on *earth*—" began Colin. Alison was

frightened and grabbed Prill's hand, and Jessie was tugging on the lead, nose to the ground, trying desperately to get away towards the road.

"It's having a fit," Oliver explained coolly. "I saw the same thing happen once, to one of our resident's cats. I know it looks frightening but that's honestly all it is. Animals do have them. The poor thing may have a tumour on its brain or something. I expect that's how it lost its ear."

"How?" said Prill, horrified.

"It must have scratched and scratched and reduced it to shreds with its claws. That'd be my guess anyway."

"It *looks* bewitched," said Colin, laughing uneasily. "Just the kind of thing an old crone like that *would* have. Heavens, I'm not going back there in a hurry."

Oliver walked ahead of his cousins, on his own. He wanted to think. His carefully reasoned explanation of the cat's crazy behaviour was only half the truth. The wretched animal may well have something wrong with its brain, but the question was, *why*? Did these fits happen all the time or had something made it happen? And had Colin's fall in the woods been just an accident, or was it something more?

Aggie Ross. She was the key. It was all very well for Colin to joke about the old crone and her cat but there'd been an awful silence when that name was mentioned. Silence you could have cut with a knife.

CHAPTER THREE

When they reached the bottom road they thought they'd better get a move on. They'd got an appointment with Hugo Grierson who was going to show them round the house. He'd told them to come at two-thirty but nobody had a watch on. It felt later than that.

They hurried past the crumbling gateposts, with their disapproving stone owls perched on top, and plunged into the gloom of the drive. It was bordered with great pine trees. The pinnacles and chimneys of the enormous house were just visible above them, and above those a dark cloud lowered. Oliver had already christened the place Castle Dracula.

"I wouldn't like to come along *here* after dark," said Colin. "No wonder the servants are always leaving. It'd give anyone the creeps. I wonder what Mr Grierson looks like? Do you think he's got fangs?"

The two boys giggled but Prill didn't join in. She wasn't at all keen on being shown round. She wanted to skip this visit and get down to the sea, to stand on a great lonely beach with nothing between her and the endless waves, taking big breaths of deep, fresh air. Lagg's woodland frightened her. There was a heaviness in the atmosphere that weighed down on her like some invisible burden, as if she'd been carrying Alison on her back for a very long time.

At the curve of the drive Aunt Phyllis met them. She was agitated and attacked them all with soap and a flannel. "This won't do at all," she snapped. "It's well past half two and Mr Grierson's been out on the steps looking for you. Now come *on*! He doesn't like to be kept waiting."

Colin really objected to the flannel treatment, but his aunt had already disappeared, dragging Oliver after her and leaving the Blakeman tribe to follow. Prill slipped away and shut Jessie up in the stone kennel outside the kitchen – Grierson wouldn't allow her to come in the house – then pelted back after the others. She found them all in the great front hall of Lagg, waiting to start the tour. Her father looked rather uneasy. Hugo Grierson seemed to have the same effect on everyone. Mr Blakeman had already told them he was a very suspicious character who didn't trust anybody and thought the whole world was out to do him down. Duncan Ross had implied that he was nothing more than a pompous old twit, and that it wasn't a castle at all. Until about ten years ago it had simply been called "Lagg", or "the big house" by the people round about. Grierson lived in it all alone "wi' naither kith nor kin", according to Granny MacCann, building up his riches, seeing no one but business people. Prill, staring up at his face from the front doorstep, thought he was the unhappiest-looking man she'd ever seen.

"An ugsome auld de'il." That's how Duncan Ross had described him. Colin found the face neither ugly nor old. Grierson was tall and rather distinguished in appearance, with silky reddish hair flecked with grey. He surely couldn't be much more than *sixty*, though he'd got a married daughter and a four-year-old grandson. Where was his wife?

"Well, you've seen the basement already, of course," he began, flashing a strained half-smile at the nervous little group. They certainly had. Dad had been given a comfortable bedroom and bathroom on the second floor, with a dressing room off it, but everyone else was below stairs. It was chilly and damp down there and the rooms were small and meanly furnished. What a place to put guests; they were more like dungeons. Perhaps Lagg Castle wasn't such a silly name after all.

Grierson explained that he couldn't spare them very much time. A business associate was due in an hour, and he had some figures to go through, so they were hurried through the hall with no time to inspect its treasures properly; the priceless-looking rugs, roped off as in some kind of stately home, the great oriental vases by the huge fireplace, the stags' heads on the walls and the feet of elephant and bison set in silver and marked with engraved brass plaques.

Colin hung back to look at a painting as the others followed Grierson up the stairs. It was labelled

"Grierson of Lagg in his old age, 1732". The face was horribly fat and the mass of greyish hair must once have been jet black. The man's skin was so dark it looked like beaten leather, but the long straight nose and the mean piggy eyes that emerged from the blubber might have belonged to Hugo Grierson himself, and he had the same thin, unforgiving mouth. Take six stone of fat away and dye his hair and this would be Grierson to the life.

No comment was made on the portrait. They climbed higher and higher, up more flights of stairs, with Grierson giving a bored running commentary on the history of the house, something he'd obviously done many times before. As they climbed, various doors were opened briefly. "The blue room... the purple room... the chintz room..." the man parrotted flatly, then, "Helen's room".

Alison saw something, tugged her hand free of her father's, and darted in. They found her clambering up on to an exquisite antique rocking horse and looking round in greedy wonder at the shelves of toys and books. She didn't want to see any more of this funny old house. Helen's room was paradise.

Grierson was looking most disapproving. Mr Blakeman quickly extracted Alison and shut the door firmly. There were loud wails all the way up to the tower suite on the fifth floor, a set of rooms where Grierson lived and where Dad was doing the portrait. She was clearly annoying Grierson. He didn't like spoiled little toddlers and that unbearable noise they all made, but she only stopped crying when they went into his private drawing room. She saw things there that made her forget the rocking horse for a while, and so did the others.

The main room was enormous. You could have made four separate ones out of it, none of them small. Doors led off it into various offices. Even in his own house Grierson talked like an estate agent. The room at the front of the house was a library, at the other end was a master bedroom, a bathroom and a dressing room. Everything was on a very grand scale.

"You could fit our whole house into this," Prill whispered to Colin. "Isn't it gloomy though?"

Off the dressing room was a second vast bedroom which had been cleared out to make a studio. Grierson disappeared into it with Dad. Now the tour was over he seemed to have forgotten all about the children and they wandered about looking at things on their own.

"For heaven's sake don't touch anything," Prill's father muttered to her as Grierson swept him off to discuss progress so far. He was obsessively interested in his portrait.

Prill went straight over to the library window with Alison in her arms. You could see the sea from there, and that was where she wanted to be, not here in this unlovely, silent house stuffed with all its dusty relics. The tide was out and the sand gleamed, peach-coloured and glistening in the afternoon sun. It was a wide, wide beach with dark woods sloping down to it, and a strip of whitish stones where the sand began. Some way out from the trees she saw a great blackened stake. It was hard to tell how tall it was, from this distance, but it looked like the trunk of a very large, straight tree, and it was driven right into the sand like a gigantic nail.

Grierson, coming through from the studio for a minute to check that nothing was being tampered with, saw her staring down. A strange, blank look came into his eyes, then his mouth twisted into a little smile. "No doubt you're wondering what *that* is? It's an old family memorial. Not ours, mind you. Now there are Rosses round here again they waste my time keeping it standing. They go down there sometimes, scraping the barnacles off. *Huh!*" He gave a loud, unpleasant laugh. "Best oak that was, from *my* woodland. Rosses... *huh*." He spat the name out as if it was poisonous.

He went back into the studio and shut the door, leaving Prill by the open window, clutching Alison, and shaking. Grierson's presence had had the most extraordinary effect on her. She'd felt almost suffocated by him, and by the sheer weight of malice and loathing in his voice. He really did seem to hate the poor Rosses, and that stake on the beach obviously had some strange significance for him. What could be wrong with the man to speak so savagely to a young girl he hardly knew?

Alison had burst into tears when she saw that thin mean face close up. She's struggled in Prill's arms and waved her little pink paws at the open window, pointing down urgently.

"Yes, *beach*," Prill murmured soothingly. "*Sand.* Allie go to beach soon. Don't cry, pet." It was better now Grierson had gone back to his precious portrait. Alison hadn't just disliked him, she'd been *scared*. Her small firm body had gone all rigid and stiff in Prill's arms, and that only ever happened when something really frightened her.

On the other side of the room Colin had made an interesting discovery. Tucked behind a cabinet, as if Grierson wanted nobody to see it, a sampler, worked in coloured wool, hung on a nail. It was the most curious text he'd ever seen on a thing like that. His grandmother had several, and they all went on about virtue and piety. But in large red letters this one stated boldy, "*Thou shalt not suffer a witch to live: Exodus 22 v. 18*", and the date was embroidered underneath in blue cross-stitch. "*May 20th 1865*".

Oliver was the person to ask about this. His general knowledge was amazing and his mother, who was very religious, had just had him confirmed. She now took him to church twice every Sunday and made him sit through extremely long services. He'd have something to say about this sampler. But when he saw what his cousin was doing Colin didn't dare call him over in case Mr Grierson suddenly came out of the studio again. The little nosy parker was bent over a large writing desk, where he actually seemed to be looking at Grierson's private papers.

What Oliver had under his nose was a diary written up for the day before, and he was busily inspecting it. Well, it couldn't be very private if the man left it open for all to see, so why not? There was nothing exciting in it anyway, just a very boring account of a very boring day, about six lines, with some additions and subtractions pencilled in the margin. What caught his eye, though, was the bit at the end in red. It was written backwards, in mirror writing, but Oliver had no problem with it. He was left-handed and he often wrote like that, when he was bored in lessons. "*Oh God,*" he read, "*wherefore art Thou absent from us so long? Why is Thy wrath so hot against the sheep of Thy pasture?*"

What on earth was that doing there? It was from one of the Psalms, one of the really miserable ones that went on and on moaning while your neck got stiff and your bottom sore, listening to the choir. Daringly, he turned back a few pages. Each entry was the same, a factual account of his day then these awful back to front bits in red. "*Haste Thee, O God, to deliver me; make haste to help me, O Lord.*" And, "*Save me, O God, for the waters are come in, even unto my soul.*"

At the sound of Grierson's voice droning on and on about canvases and poses and what he ought to wear for his portrait, Oliver retreated hastily and whipped round. Colin stepped back from the queer sampler and pretended to be inspecting a clock, and Prill came forward into the middle of the room with Alison held in front of her, like a shield. In Grierson's presence they all lined up automatically, like an army waiting for instructions.

He came over to the window, pushed past Prill, stood looking out for a minute, then slammed it shut quite violently. It was as if he'd seen or heard something down there that displeased him. He even drew a curtain half-way across and darkened the room. All sense of peace had vanished with his coming, and as soon as she saw him, Alison began to cry bitterly. He clearly wanted them out of the way. An accountant called Robert Guthrie was due, and Dad had been asked to stay for a drink so they could meet each other, and have a look at the portrait together.

The children were offered nothing, and Mr Grierson was steering them testily towards some cold back stairs.

"You'll get down quicker that way," he said stiffly, almost pushing them through the door. Alison was now crying quite hysterically. She was cold out here and she wanted to stay with her father.

"Never mind, pet," Prill said, stroking her cheek. "He's a horrid man, he doesn't understand about families. Don't cry. We can take you down to the beach."

"No wonder his daughter married and left home," Colin whispered to Oliver as they clattered down the icy stone staircase. "No wonder she never comes to see him. Can't blame her. Can you?"

CHAPTER FOUR

"You *can* go," said Aunt Phyllis, "as long as you're back by six. No, no, leave Alison with me. Don't want any disasters. Now about the swimming—"

"Mother, we aren't *going* swimming," Oliver said impatiently. "I've told you, we just want to have a look at the beach, that's all."

"We saw it from Mr Grierson's room," added Prill. "It looks beautiful."

"All right then." Aunt Phyllis sounded distinctly put out. She'd decided to make them all tidy up their rooms before the evening meal. The Blakemans didn't put anything away, and there were books all over Oliver's bed. Still, it was a fine afternoon, and there may not be too many of those. Let them go to their beach. It'd be quieter anyway, with just the toddler to cope with.

Prill half ran there, partly because she was trying to keep up with Jessie, partly because she wanted to escape from Lagg's woodlands and get by the sea. At least Grierson didn't own that. When the two boys caught up with her she was standing quite still on the edge of the plantation. The trees were small here and many were half buried in fine sand. It was such an exposed stretch of coast Prill wondered how anything could survive for very long. Except on the calmest day the winds rushed across wildly and the currents were highly dangerous, according to Duncan, the tide creeping up quite without warning. There were ugly "No Swimming" notices all along the dunes, at lurching angles, like old gravestones.

Colin and Oliver came up behind and stared with her. Directly in front of them, stretching for miles on each side, were the most marvellous dunes. The sand was silver-white, so clean you could almost smell it, and moulded into great mounds and hollows by the endless wind that had made holes and dips and craters in it, like the surface of the moon.

Colin wished he was six again. He wanted to kick his shoes off and roll in those hollows, he wanted to tear away and hide, he wanted to run to the very tops and pelt down the sandy slopes and plop into the bottom like a baby. But Oliver's eyes saw none of this. They were riveted on the stake.

"Let's walk out to it," he said in an odd, faraway voice. "Let's get there before the tide comes in. I want to see it properly."

"Oh, it'll be hours before we need to worry about that," said Colin, clambering down through the dunes and on to the flat of the beach. "It's not turned yet, surely."

"It has, you know, and it comes up quite suddenly just here. Your friend Duncan said so." Oliver's voice was sarcastic. He was a bit sick of hearing all about what Duncan Ross said and did. Colin so obviously preferred the Scots boy to him. "Come on Prill," he called. She was still up on the dunes, throwing sticks to Jessie. "We don't want to go back without seeing it."

Prill came, reluctantly. It was a beautiful beach but the stake spoiled it. Unless you hid in one of the moon craters there was nowhere you could go without your eye catching it. Its knobbled blackness reared up, staining the pure sand, and made strange witchy shadows as the afternoon sun sank lower, and the first chill of the evening crept up on them.

"It's much bigger than it looks," said Oliver, crouching down, "Thicker as well as taller." They were right up to the stake now, and wandering all round it. "And it's pine, not oak," he added, squinting at it.

"Grierson said it was *oak*," Prill muttered, standing away from it. "Best oak from my own woodland," she repeated. "That's what he said."

"Well, the first one must have been oak in that case," said Oliver, taking a tape measure from his pocket. "But, if the site's as old as people think, it must have been replaced several times."

"How long has it been here then?" asked Colin.

"Oh, hundreds of years. I don't know exactly. I've not researched it properly yet," his cousin said self-importantly, measuring the girth of the trunk. "How tall do you think it is?"

Colin stood next to it. "Well, I'm five foot six, so I

reckon… one… two… about eight feet, say eight and a half. But what's it *doing* here? That's what I'd like to know."

"Dunno. We can ask the Rosses. They look after it," said Oliver, "according to Drac. It obviously marks some significant event though. Perhaps it was the scene of a fight or something. We're quite near the English border here after all." He pocketed his tape measure, folded his arms and stared at it thoughtfully. Prill had her back to the two boys and was leaning against the stake, staring out to sea.

"The tide *is* coming in," she said dreamily. "Look, it's filling all these little channels now. We'll get our feet wet if we don't budge."

Colin suddenly whispered something to Oliver and the boy smiled, and dug in his pocket. A minute later poor Prill found herself grabbed from behind and tied securely to the old wooden stump with a green tape measure. The others were running off up the beach. Jessie was leaping about, pawing and slobbering all over her, and the tide was filling those deep channels faster and faster.

"Come *back*!" she screamed, tugging at the tape. "Don't be so foul, you two. It's not funny. This thing's really tight… I'm getting wet. Oh, come *on*."

She didn't want to do an Oliver and be a spoilsport, though it was rather typical of him to lend his tape measure for a trick he'd have hated himself. But Prill

41

didn't like it. The tide *was* coming in, and the bumps and knobbles of the slimy black stake were digging into her back. "*Colin!*" she yelled, starting to panic.

"All right, all right. Hang on Joan of Arc." He came racing back. He knew Prill was rather thin-skinned about practical jokes. They were both ankle-deep in water now while the cowardly Oliver was striding off firmly towards the dunes. "Sorry," he muttered, as Prill stood there crossly, lashed to the great wooden stump with her brother picking at the knots. "I didn't mean to tie it quite so tightly... *there*."

She was free, rubbing her wrists and trying to find a bit of sandbank to stand on, to escape from the swirling water. "Trying to drown me, were you? And listen to Oliver, he's laughing at us. He's an absolute pig. I'll tie him up, next time."

"Nobody's laughing," Colin said quietly. "Don't over-react. He's just embarrassed because it was his tape."

"He *is* laughing," Prill interrupted angrily, starting to run. "Just wait till I get hold of him." She began to chase up the beach after the skinny retreating figure in its baggy shorts.

Colin stared after them, and the laughter came again, on the wind. The sound sent an icy chill through him. Prill was quite right, someone *had* laughed at her as she stood lashed to the stake with Oliver's tape measure, and they were laughing now. But it was a thin, high-pitched screaming kind of laugh, not Oliver's voice at all. He'd heard it before. It was the laughter he'd heard in the woodland when the barrow tipped over and the stones hurt his foot.

CHAPTER FIVE

It was just half past nine. Oliver had been writing his diary and he was now in the bathroom, going through his elaborate bedtime ritual of cleaning his teeth and brushing his hair one hundred times. His mother believed it was the only sure way of avoiding nits.

He called his diary a journal, but it wasn't a grand leather-bound affair like Hugo Grierson's, just a small Woolworth's exercise book, and he didn't write in it every day. It was kept for events of special importance in his life. There'd been quite a lot to say, tonight.

"*This holiday's going to be lonely for me*," read Colin. He'd come to talk to Oliver and found the bedroom empty and the notebook open on a table. Down the passage he could hear his cousin making splashing noises at the washbasin. Guiltily, Colin read on.

"*They never take much notice of me,*" the account continued, "*but now they've made friends with Duncan Ross it's going to be even worse. He's just Colin's type, big and sporty. They even look alike. Daren't think what they say about me, when I'm not there.*"

Colin and Prill were rather attractive children, and poor Oliver was only too aware that he was a bit funny-looking. Colin was tall and broad, with a handsome mop of auburn hair, and Prill was growing more and more like something out of a Victorian painting. She had red hair too, and she wore it long. Both had large brown eyes and the kind of skin that tanned easily. People sometimes commented on their good looks in Oliver's presence. He didn't think it was very tactful. They did quite well in school and they were both good swimmers, whereas Oliver swam like a brick. Colin was getting good at rugby too, according to his father. "*Where was I when all the prizes were given out?*" Oliver had written bitterly, thinking about those great beefy shoulders. "*I can't help being small for my age,*" the spindly writing went on, "*and I was very ill when I was little. That can weaken you for life. Those two never think about that of course. I couldn't have lifted those stones at Lochashiel even if I'd wanted to (WHICH I DIDN'T), and anyway, those bones I dug up from the mud may be extremely important. Not sure I'll show them though.*"

Colin, feeling more and more uncomfortable, turned the page in fascination. "*What I really ought to find out is—*"

"Seen enough?" said a spiteful little voice from the doorway. Oliver was wearing striped Viyella pyjamas and carrying a large sponge-bag, and his thin face was dark pink with rage. He stormed across the room and snatched the notebook from Colin's fingers with such force that it ripped across the back. "Do you make a habit of reading other people's diaries, Colin?" he spat out, in a strangled voice.

"No more than you do," his cousin answered smartly. "You were reading Mr Grierson's. I saw you."

There was an abrupt silence, and Oliver flushed darker than ever. "That was different," he stammered. "There's something going on here. It involves Mr Grierson, and we've got to get to the bottom of it."

"I know," Colin said quietly. "That's why I've come. Prill's coming too, in a minute."

The two boys stared at one another. Oliver had lost his usual composure and his face had somehow crumpled up. He actually looked as if he might cry, when he saw the ripped notebook.

Colin felt rather sorry for him, and he hated himself for having read the diary. At least he knew how things looked to Oliver.

"I'm sorry, Oll," he said. "I shouldn't have read your diary and... and we didn't *mean* to be unfriendly."

There was a pause, then Colin said awkwardly, "Well, what was *in* Grierson's diary, anything important?"

Oliver shrugged. "It was all a bit boring really, with sums down the margin. He obviously studies his bank balance when there's not much to say. That's the *real* sign of a miser."

"Anything else?" said Colin, trying to sound casual. The familiar faraway expression in Oliver's eyes told him that there *was*.

"Yes, as a matter of fact," his cousin replied, in rather a grand voice. He knew Colin was dying to know.

"He'd written something from the bible, in red, after every single entry. And he'd written it *backwards*."

"Could you work it out?" Colin asked, more and more intrigued.

"Oh yes," Oliver said airily. "Easy as anything. It's mirror writing. Anyone can do it, once they've got the knack."

"Go on then, what did it say?"

" 'Oh God, wherefore art thou absent from us so long'," quoted Oliver. " 'Save me, for the waters have entered my soul'. Things like that. They were all the same, all about being cut off from the land of the living."

"Heavens," Colin muttered dumbly. "Why write that sort of thing in a diary?"

Oliver pulled a face. "Search me. Perhaps he's brooding over something... perhaps he feels guilty. He *looks* guilty, don't you think? He's got that shifty look round his eyes."

Colin tried to recall Grierson's face. They'd only seen the man once. "I don't know," he said thoughtfully. I thought he was rather striking, as a matter of fact, but definitely unhappy-looking. Why write backwards though? That's *bizarre*."

"Witches did things back to front," Oliver said solemnly. "To undo the power of good."

"Oh *Oll*, surely you're not saying—"

"I'm not saying anything, yet," the boy cut in impatiently. "I'm just telling you they did, that's all. It's worth remembering."

There was a sudden tap on the door.

"That'll be Prill," Colin said, whispering just in case Aunt Phyllis was creeping about somewhere. "She wanted to talk to you as well."

"Wait a minute." Spread over Oliver's bed was a navy-blue T-shirt with a collection of small bones on it. They were arranged in a definite pattern but Oliver had scooped them all up into a polythene bag before Colin could stop him.

"What did you do that for?" he said in frustration. "You said they were *important*, in – in your diary..." He went red.

"Not sure about them yet," Oliver replied curtly. "Anyway, Prill's squeamish. *Don't go on about them.*" He shoved the bag under his pillow.

"Mr Grierson's out there," Prill said in a low voice, coming inside and shutting the door firmly. "I was just leaving my room, and I saw him. What's *he* doing down here?"

"Eavesdropping probably," Colin muttered. "We think there's something peculiar about him."

"You can say that again. I think he's more than peculiar, I think he's *unhinged*. He's so violent, when he speaks to you, he sort of *hisses*. Allie's absolutely terrified of him."

"He's got the devil in him," Oliver announced flatly. "Duncan Ross said that, and for once I agree with him."

The other two stared at him. "You don't mean *literally*, Oll? What on earth are you talking about?" Colin said at last.

"I don't know, quite," Oliver said evenly, cupping his chin in his hands. "I just know there's something wrong here, but I'm not at all sure it's his *fault*. This awful behaviour's not really typical apparently. He doesn't usually rage *quite* so much at people, according to what Ma's heard from Granny MacCann. He's always been a loner, at least, he has since his wife died."

"Well, he's foul to the Rosses," Colin said quietly. "Really foul."

Oliver didn't reply, he was obviously thinking about what might have soured the man, over the years. "His wife fell off a horse and was killed," he informed them, "when their child was four."

"Helen," Prill murmured sadly, remembering the rocking-horse room.

"Yes, Helen. Well, that can't have been much fun for him, being left on his own and everything, and he's fallen out with her now, because she married someone he didn't approve of. Then there's the potty old mother, he looked after her for years and years. When he was a boy she used to drive him to church three times every Sunday, and make him learn great chunks of the Bible off by heart. If he got anything wrong she hit him. Well, that's what Granny MacCann told Ma. No wonder he never goes to church these days."

Colin and Prill exchanged sly glances. It sounded so like Oliver, an elderly religious mother, and being forced to go to church, and having to learn pieces of the Bible. Aunt Phyllis did that to him.

Oliver was still thinking of those red back to front bits in Grierson's diary but he kept silent. Hugo Grierson had chosen the most agonized verses of the Psalms he could think of. Nothing cheerful like "Make a joyful noise unto the Lord" or "The Lord is My Shepherd". He *must* be deeply guilty about something. What had he done? Had he got rich by embezzling other people's money, or had he killed somebody? Lagg Castle was a perfect place for a murder, all those echoing corridors, all those pine forests outside, to hide the body in...

"Why were you so against those stones being moved, Oll?" Colin's voice jerked him back to reality. "We could see you didn't want them touched. That's why we've come, really."

"*And* because of what went on in the forest," Oliver added firmly. "You'd better tell me what did happen, hadn't you? I mean when you were on your own."

Their ten year old cousin, undersized and feeble, now spoke with immense authority. There had been moments like this before, times when they almost feared Oliver, times when those curious pale eyes of his saw so much more in events than the eyes of ordinary people.

"Someone jumped on my back," Colin said blankly, going cold at the very thought of it. "Someone I couldn't see leapt on me, and dug their fingers into my neck, and... they were so light and quick about it I – I thought it was you."

He expected some outraged response from poor Oliver who'd already had his diary read, and his private thoughts laid bare, but the boy didn't seem at all angry. His face had darkened and he was obviously pursuing rather a different line of thought.

"So she is out," he said, in a small voice, and he scratched his head thoughtfully.

"*Who's* 'out'?" demanded Prill, bewildered.

"Aggie Ross."

"Oh, *Oll*," Colin said impatiently. "That's nuts. We've no *idea* who Aggie Ross is. She may just be some crony of Granny MacCann's, or a relation of Duncan's, for all we know."

"And you can't take what *she* says too seriously," Prill chipped in. "I mean she's so doddery. She's probably wandering in her mind. Old people like her get all kinds of weird ideas."

"She seemed perfectly sane and sensible to me," Oliver said coldly, remembering how the Blakemans had cracked jokes about her being a witch. " '*Thou shalt not suffer a witch to live*'," he said aloud. "Wonder how that comes into it?"

Colin looked at him keenly. "I saw that too. It was embroidered on that sampler behind the cabinet."

"Perhaps Aggie Ross was a witch," mutter

"And perhaps that cairn was the remains of her house."

"And we've broken into it," Colin said, "and set her free. Is that what you're getting at?"

"Could be."

There was a long embarrassed silence. Oliver had had strange ideas before, but this was fantastic.

"If I'm right," he went on, talking more to himself than to the others, "she won't leave us alone. Something else will happen. You'll see. Unless of course we take all the stones back again."

Colin stared at him. He could just imagine what Angus Ross would say if a small boy asked him to dismantle a newly-repaired stone wall, to pacify a non-existent witch.

They were still sitting there, looking at one another in blank confusion, when the door burst open and Aunt Phyllis appeared. She was not pleased.

"Ten thirty," she snapped, consulting her watch. "What's this, may I ask? A mothers' meeting? Colin, Prill, off to bed at once! Lights out, Oliver, you know the rules. Have you cleaned your teeth?"

"Yes, Mother," said a muffled voice from under the eiderdown. "*And* brushed my hair."

He listened to Colin's door bang shut, then to Prill's. Ten minutes later he heard his mother climb into bed. They had adjoining rooms and the walls were very thin, only plasterboard partitions dividing up what had once been a vast storage area in the basement.

Soon she was snoring steadily. Oliver got out his diary, switched a little torch on, and re-read it. Then he lay back, thinking about witches, and about Aggie Ross and Granny MacCann.

Ma wouldn't let him read spooky books, and she'd be very disturbed if she thought that he was getting seriously interested in witchcraft. She was a devout woman and the Bible warned against meddling with what it called "the powers of darkness". But the text *was* there, on that sampler. What could it mean?

"*Save me, Oh God, for the waters are come in, unto my soul.*" Oliver had written it down in small neat capitals. The words filled him with sadness for Hugo Grierson, shut up all alone in this ugly old house. Why did he torment himself so? And why did he use mirror-writing? That struck him as extremely peculiar. Witches did things backwards. It seemed that the beauty of the sea and the woodlands of Lagg, instead of gladdening the man's heart plunged him into black despair. It was a lovely place, but there was a kind of brooding sorrow about it all.

Oliver was tired, but he always read a little at night, to get himself off to sleep. He grinned as he heard his mother's even snoring, and shone his high intensity pocket torch on the pages of his book. He'd smuggled it up here without her seeing it. It was *The Bumper Annual of Great Horror Stories.*

CHAPTER SIX

At the other end of the stone passage Prill had just sat up in bed. She was annoyed because it had taken her a long time to get off to sleep after that conversation with Oliver, and her hot water bottle had gone cold – a hot water bottle in *August* – but it was chilly in the dungeons at night. Then, just as she was drifting off at last, Aunt Phyllis had woken her up again.

When she'd opened her eyes she'd been dimly aware of footsteps coming and going, shuffling sort of steps, the kind you make if you slither along in flat rubber shoes. Aunt Phyllis had several pairs. She was obsessed about not making any unnecessary noise. Then Prill heard her singing softly to herself.

What on earth was the woman doing? She'd go mad if any of the children went round singing at one in the morning. She'd report it to the management (Dad), who'd warned them all that Mr Grierson was a funny customer and had to be handled with care. Yet here she was, singing at dead of night, and creeping up and down. Was she looking under all their doors, perhaps, to check that they'd obeyed lights out? Prill couldn't understand it.

As she listened, though, she realized that it couldn't

be her aunt singing. It must be the radio, or a tape perhaps. But that didn't make sense. Nobody had brought a tape recorder and they certainly didn't broadcast church services in the middle of the night... Prill began to feel uneasy.

She crept out of bed, stood in the middle of the room, and listened carefully. The voice was a woman's, young and sweet, and it had a distinct Scots accent. She was singing a hymn, very slowly and mournfully, something Prill had never heard before:

> "*Let not the errors of my youth*
> *Or sins remembered be.*
> *In mercy, for Thy goodness' sake,*
> *O Lord, remember me...*"

The words were very clear but at the end there was a broken sound, as if the singer had struggled hard with some deep emotion, and lost. Slowly the singing turned into weeping, and the soft shuffling steps went on, to and fro, somewhere very close to her.

But not on the other side of the door. The singer was in the open air, walking relentlessly up and down in the cold wet grass. There was no curtain at the window, and through it Prill saw something, not a face, but a pale white arm, and a hand stretched out in supplication.

She made a dive for the bedclothes and pulled them up over her head, shaking it violently from side to side, to get rid of the ghostly voice, and screwing up her eyes to blot out the picture of that pale, beseeching hand. The window was actually open a few inches – Aunt Phyllis had insisted, and gone round checking at bedtime. Perhaps if she shut it, firmly and noisily, whoever it was out there would be frightened away.

After a few minutes, her heart crashing against her ribs, Prill emerged from the bedding and tiptoed across the room. The window was a square of black and the voice had stopped. So had the shuffling footsteps. Her violent movement must have been seen, through the glass, and scared whoever it was away. She'd better tell someone in the morning. It must be some simple-minded soul that wandered about in Lagg's grounds in the small hours. Whoever it was couldn't be out to scare people, not singing sad little hymn tunes like that, and just walking about in the grass.

Feeling a little calmer, Prill pulled the window towards her and fastened it carefully, shutting out the sweet night smell of the garden, and also a comfortable animal smell that had drifted into the room as she stood listening to the strange, broken little voice. Then she got into bed again, did a bit of cycling to warm herself up, and fell soundly asleep almost at once.

Up in his tower rooms Hugo Grierson was horribly awake, still fully clothed, and sitting at his writing desk. There was a full moon and he was looking out across the dense carpet of woodland to a wide expanse of silvery beach. The tide was ebbing again, and the black stake in the sand came up through the shining water like the arm of a man drowning. There was a wind, and puffs of cloud flitted across the moon's face making everything move eerily, making the stake move, as if the arm was waving, or clutching out at some invisible rescuer.

Grierson shut his eyes and clapped his hands over his ears. All the windows were shut, and the lonely beach a good two miles away, but he could hear the voice quite loudly, as if she was in the room with him.

> *"Sweet Jesus, in Thy mercy's sake,*
> *Sweet Lord, remember me…"*

It had begun again, he'd heard it quite plainly that afternoon, when those kids were up in his rooms. The voice that came to him from the shore, through the forest, across the fields and gardens, was only the beginning. It would not always be calm and sweet. There would be agonized shrieks, sobbings and screamings that only he could hear. He pulled all the curtains across, blotting out the bright moon, strode across the library, through the shadowy drawing room, and sat down on his bed. But inside his head the singing went on and on, mournful and quiet, like the soughing of some distant sea.

There would be no end to it. The two Rosses were at

the heart of this, and nothing would ever convince him otherwise. If they went out of his life he would surely have peace again? All alone in his great rooms, arrogant, rich Hugo Grierson buried his face in his hands and sobbed like a little child.

CHAPTER SEVEN

Both Prill and Oliver found it hard to get up the next morning. When, eventually, they trailed bleary-eyed into the kitchen they found everyone else had already breakfasted and scattered. Mr Blakeman was up in the studio and Alison was sitting on the floor, cheerfully banging pan lids together. Colin had gone down to the field, to watch Duncan and his father repair the wall.

Aunt Phyllis was snappy. "Don't blame *me* if your boiled eggs are hard," she said. "I called you and called you. And don't blame *me* if your cornflakes are soggy. It's your own fault."

You didn't *have* to put the milk on for us, Prill thought in disgust, turning over the brown mush with a spoon. Sometimes she thought Aunt Phyllis did such things on purpose, as a kind of punishment. She pitied Oliver.

He grinned at her as he ate his egg. "Take no notice," he whispered. "Mornings are her worst time. She's getting herself *organized*. She doesn't mean it really."

You could have fooled me, thought Prill, chewing on the leathery boiled egg. *Ugh,* it was horrible, but she didn't dare leave it. Aunt Phyllis was now on the phone in the stone lobby, busily informing the local baker that she wouldn't be wanting him to call for the next few weeks.

"I always bake my *own* bread," she was saying emphatically. "What? *What?* Speak up, man. Oh no, no cakes or buns, nothing like that, thank you."

Prill pitied the baker. It'd be all round Kirkmichael by dinner time, how Grierson's new housekeeper had stopped the order from the Big House. Granny MacCann was probably telling somebody about it at this very minute.

"She *does* look like a witch, Oll," she said dreamily.

"Who? My mother? Well honestly…"

"No, twit. *Granny MacCann.* She does, you've got to admit it."

"Well, I dare say you would, if you'd lost nearly all your teeth, and your face had shrivelled up like that. It's not her fault, she's old."

"No, but…" Prill's voice dried up.

In silence she watched her cousin turn his empty eggshell upside down and smash it to smithereens with a spoon.

"*There*," he said. "Now the witches can't have it."

"What do you mean?"

"Ah well," he confided. "You've got to do that because otherwise they might sail away in them. Didn't you know?" he added disparagingly. "They use sieves too."

Oliver's head was stuffed with strange and curious facts. He was hopeless at games and a real loner in the form room, but he always came top of the class because he had such a phenomenal memory. Prill had wanted to talk to someone about Granny MacCann, about the horrible sick cat and the heaps of bones in that smelly room. She also wanted to tell someone about what she had seen last night, but somehow she didn't think Oliver would be very sympathetic. People were always telling her not to be fanciful. Even Oliver might think she'd imagined it all. He was always so matter of fact.

Aunt Phyllis made them wash up their breakfast things and got Oliver to put some coal on the fire. She was determined to have *one* warm room in this basement. Then she gave them a rucksack containing food for the day. They were actually being let off the leash for a few hours.

"Get some colour in those cheeks," she bossed, fitting the straps over Oliver's shoulders. "Breathe in some of this marvellous air. It's like wine."

"What are *you* doing, Auntie Phyllis?" asked Prill. "And what about Alison?"

"I'm baking today. Alison can help me. Don't worry about her."

Prill wasn't worrying, but she'd rather hoped to bring Alison on the picnic too. Aunt Phyllis had other plans for the morning, though, and that was that, apparently.

A string of instructions followed them down the path to the field, where they were going to collect Colin. Not Striking Any Matches, Keeping That Dog Under Strict Control, No Swimming Near The Stake. "And keep to the *paths*" was the final command.

Wipe your feet upon the mat, fold your pyjamas, clean your teeth with the paste provided... honestly, she was just like a gramophone record, thought Prill, following Oliver down the track. No wonder he was a bit weird, having to put up with that all day long.

Their plan was to find the castle on the island. The locals called it Hag's Folly, according to Duncan.

"It sounds awful," Prill said, as they walked along. "Mad Hag's House I'm going to call it." Folly meant foolishness, didn't it? Maybe the strange shape she'd seen in the night was a local character. The poor girl must be simple in the head. They might even meet her, wandering about in the woods.

Oliver was reading from a little pamphlet as they went along. "A folly's a sham tower according to this," he said owlishly. "So it's wrong, because the place is ancient. Six hundred years old at least, and hag... hag," he muttered, turning the page. "Hag means crone or witch. There you are, Prill, we just can't get away from them."

"Sure it's not *Haggis's* Castle, Oll?" Colin said, winking at Prill. "That sounds more Scottish to me."

Oliver had opened his mouth to deliver a stinging

reply when he shut it again abruptly. The dense woodland had thinned quite suddenly. Sunlight was filtering through the trees, and the path had petered out into a small rocky shore. They were standing on the edge of a tiny loch, ringed three-quarters round by dark pines but with low grey-green hills directly opposite, forming a gentle backcloth. In the middle of the loch they saw a small island and on it a square grey tower, mantled on one side with ivy that swept down from crumbling battlements like a lock of falling hair.

Nobody spoke. The silence of the place was magical, nothing broke it, not even the odd bird that winged now and then across the bluish water, or the wind that stirred the pines at the lake's edge. It was all so small and so perfect, a secret place to be stored up in the memory, a lovely place, one never to be shared with those who did not understand. They all felt it as they stood there in silence, staring across at the ruined tower, longing to reach it.

Where the low hills met the water a silver thread ran down and dropped into the lake. "It's fed by that burn," said Oliver. "It's quite full, considering there's been so little rain."

The stream made a ripple where its waters entered the loch. Colin trained his binoculars on it. "It's bigger than it looks," he said. "There's quite a current out there. You'd have to be careful in a boat."

"But there isn't one," Prill said flatly.

"Oh, there must be. This is still Mr Grierson's land, don't forget. He'll have something to get across in, even if it's just a holey old dinghy," Colin replied, setting off along a sandy path that seemed to go round the loch.

About a hundred yards on they found the boat with someone already at the oars. An old man all muffled up in a plaid as if it were mid-winter, with everything hidden except two bright blue eyes and a forelock of fuzzy white hair. Prill stared at him nervously. The sunlight still danced on the water but there was a sudden chill in the air. She pulled at the open neck of her shirt, buttoning it right up as shivers crept down her back.

Jessie clearly didn't want to go on the boat at all. She whined and tugged at the lead, almost dragging Prill backwards into the forest.

"*Quiet,* girl! *Behave!*" Colin shouted, tapping her smartly on the nose. The old man might not take them if she played up, and there seemed to be no other way of getting across. "Has anyone any cash?" he said, looking at the others. The weird old man hadn't addressed a single word to them yet, but he'd cleared a space in the boat and a brown, claw-like hand had been thrust under Colin's nose.

Prill had no pockets in her summer skirt, but Oliver found twenty pence in his jeans, and Colin had a pound coin in his. He laid the pieces flat in his palm, and held them out. "This is all we've got, I'm afraid. Will this be enough for a return journey, us three and the dog?"

Jessie was whining and cringing so much they expected the old man to refuse to take her, but he snatched the coins and immediately waved them aboard with one thin, horny hand, making the dog lie flat in the bottom of the boat. Almost at once they found themselves gliding steadily across the still, dark waters towards Hag's Folly.

They soon gave up trying to talk to the old man. Either he was deaf and dumb, or just plain hostile. He ignored everything they said but simply rowed on, steady and silent, like some well-oiled machine. It was hard to believe that anyone so ancient and hunched-looking could be so strong.

Where the burn flowed into the loch the water was quite choppy and the boat rocked about. Jessie, who'd been growling at the old man, now started to bark hysterically and actually tried to leap out. Prill ended up sitting on the floor of the dinghy with the dog in her lap, making soothing noises.

The old man simply rowed on. The plaid had half fallen away from his head, revealing a bony face tanned to the colour of a ripe chestnut, but there was an odd smoothness about the skin. For someone so old it was a curiously unwrinkled face. The flesh was stretched tightly across it, giving it a haunted, skeletal quality. All three were disconcerted by what they saw; they looked, but only for a moment, then turned away.

Now the water was calm again the dog settled down

and Prill was able to take her seat and stare across at the island. Oliver was prattling away from his pamphlet, while Colin had his binoculars trained upwards. Duncan had said there were golden eagles round here.

Jessie was making her happy, growly noise, as if someone was patting her, and pulling at her silky ears. Once or twice Prill turned round, looking beyond the old man to the empty seat in the back. It had fishing tackle on it, and Oliver's green rucksack, but Prill had an uncanny, ridiculous sense of someone else being in the boat with them, someone the dog approved of, whose warm country smell was mingling with the smell of the pines. It was the smell she'd noticed in her room, last night.

As soon as the boat scraped shingle the three children were bundled off the boat and the old man turned his back on them, silently rearranging his oars. Oliver was already halfway to the tower, pamphlet in hand, and Prill had pelted after Jessie who'd leapt ashore first and disappeared into the ruin. Colin hoped the old boatman wouldn't be too difficult about the return trip. They hadn't got any more money. If he wanted more, they'd have to come back with it tomorrow.

"We're going to stay for a bit," he said, "and have our sandwiches." He was looking at the ground because the brown skeletal face frightened him so much. "Could you come back for us, in a couple of hours say? If it's no trouble, of course…"

There was no answer, and when Colin looked up the boat was already well out from the shore with that hunched figure rowing strongly away across the black silent water.

"*Hey!*" Colin shouted, dancing up and down in panic then cupping his hands to his mouth. "*Hey!* Stop, will you! What on earth have you left us here for? Come *back*! How are we supposed to get home?"

CHAPTER EIGHT

In her dungeon kitchen, back at Castle Dracula, poor Aunt Phyllis was having a very bad time. She soon regretted her generous offer to have Alison for the morning while Mr Blakeman had a long session on the portrait. The angelic-looking toddler was turning out to be a real demon. Her aunt was used to well-regulated children, not little beasts like this.

To begin with, she would keep blowing out the pilot light in the oven. It was a filthy old thing, and Aunt Phyllis was desperately trying to get it hot enough for bread-making. There was a small cast-iron door through which you pushed a lighted taper, at the same time holding a knob down with your finger while you counted to ten. After three or four useless attempts Aunt Phyllis got the knack. Manufacturer's instructions were always hopeless anyway. She held the red knob down and sang a whole verse of *To Be A Pilgrim* as she did so. That did the trick. This time the pilot light stayed on. Now she turned a big black knob fully anti-clockwise, as instructed, and with a little roar all the rusty burners suddenly burst into life.

But the stove hadn't been on five minutes when fizzle, pop, the whole thing went out again with a dismal splutter, and she caught Alison lying flat on the kitchen floor, peeping curiously through the fascinating spyhole.

"Gone," she said blandly. "Fire gone." She was very disappointed not to see the fizzling, popping flames any more.

"Naughty, *naughty* girl!" Aunt Phyllis said impatiently, yanking her away from the oven, standing her upright and brushing her down. The wretched child was covered in fine black dust. She must have blown the pilot out, and after all that palaver of getting it lit.

"Now you sit there, my girl," she said sharply. "You draw a nice pattern for Daddy." She settled Alison on a stool at the kitchen table and laid out the paper and chubby crayons Mrs Blakeman had sent in Prill's suitcase, then she went through the whole ritual of lighting the stove all over again. This time she got to verse three before the monstrous contraption stayed on. "Since, Lord, Thou dost defend Us with Thy spirit," she warbled in her thin, rather reedy voice, gingerly releasing the red knob and turning the black one. Success at last. This time the stove did stay on, and Aunt Phyllis turned to her bread-making in a slightly better humour.

She'd only just started the kneading process when splutter, pop, the burners went out yet again, and there was the wicked little girl lying on the floor in precisely the same position as before, peering through the spy-hole and thoughtfully chewing a crayon. "Gone," she bleated, "all gone."

Aunt Phyllis could have throttled her. She *did* smack her, very smartly on both hands. "Naughty girl," she said again. "Naughty, *very* naughty, to blow the fire out after all Auntie's trouble."

Alison burst into loud sobs, looking in bewilderment at her red palms. "Allie not blow," she howled. The poor little girl was so outraged that, just for a minute, Aunt Phyllis did wonder. There was really no good reason for that stove going out. It had apparently been serviced the day before they'd arrived.

"Come on, girlie," she said, rather more kindly. "Take these out into the sunshine, then you won't get under Auntie's feet. These are your cousin Oliver's." She produced a shoe box full of small, battered cars, and the snivelling toddler followed her outside. Aunt Phyllis propped the door open with a chair so Alison could run in and out, then crouched down yet again, on the kitchen floor, with matches and spills to attack the stove. But in the course of the morning it went out four times, and at no point was Alison anywhere near it. To her that oven meant shouting, and Big Smacks. She didn't like the peephole any more.

Aunt Phyllis was cold in the kitchen in spite of the coal fire. Her back was all shivery and she felt curiously sluggish as she pottered around, bowed-down almost by the weight of her fifty-odd years. Today they felt much more. She'd have to get the kettle going, and make a strong cup of tea.

She hummed as she went round, snatches of hymns and little scraps of the Psalms. Uncle Stanley wasn't a Believer so she never sang when he was around, but here there was nobody to object, except little Alison, and she was outside with Oliver's cars, babbling away gravely to a dented London bus. She obviously didn't like the humming though. Every time Aunt Phyllis started a new tune she made a growling noise; sometimes it became quite loud. Once the poor woman turned round to tell her off, the disapproving noise was so distinct – it was never too early to teach the young good manners – but no, there she was, flat out on the warm path, lining up all the "poor cars" to take them to hospital.

A certain uneasiness had started to gnaw at the practical, no-nonsense Aunt Phyllis. She'd simply refused to take Granny MacCann's gloomy stories of Lagg Castle seriously, or the old woman's unshaken belief that there was a badness in it that came "frae the de'il his-sel". Those were wicked, evil thoughts, forgivable only because Granny was so very old and confused. But she herself had to admit she didn't really care for the general atmosphere of the place, not today anyway. She comforted herself with the teapot and sat drinking at the kitchen table from a handsome willow-pattern cup. She was pouring out her second, and actually warming up a little, when naughty Alison threw a great handful of gravel in at the door, chipping the teapot and actually breaking the cup.

In a rage, Aunt Phyllis shot to her feet, knocking her chair over as she did so, and charged to the door. The hospital session was over and the cars neatly ranged round, as if for a tea party. Alison lay on the path waving her fat little legs in the air, quite oblivious of her aunt's presence.

Aunt Phyllis looked round carefully. There wasn't a trace of gravel on the smooth tarmac path, nothing by the back door but a clump of small rowan trees set in freshly-turned earth. Angus Ross had been weeding in the kitchen garden the day before.

Very slowly, still looking all round, she went back inside. The queer heaviness in her shoulders was becoming more general. In fact it was turning into a thumping headache. If she didn't take one of her pills quickly she was going to have a migraine attack. Could she have imagined that gravel? *No she could not.* There it was, all over the clean kitchen floor. Bits of it had even landed in the dough, rising at last in a pan on the old gas stove.

She was just foraging in her handbag for her pink pills when there was a sudden almighty crash, and a tinkling of glass. The tumbler of water on the table went hurtling to the ground and smashed into several pieces, and her pan of dough went flying off the stove and landed in the open doorway.

The noise brought Alison rushing in. She clearly didn't like it. "Bear," she whimpered nervously, peeping all round the kitchen and clinging to her aunt's apron. "Allie not like bear."

Under the kitchen table was a huge white stone, almost too heavy to lift. Aunt Phyllis was shaking violently but she knew that she mustn't break down in front of the child.

"A naughty boy has done this," she announced, sounding a lot calmer than she felt, "A *very* naughty boy who wants to make Mr Grierson *very* cross."

She spread a newspaper out on the table and lifted the white boulder on to it. There was her evidence, and there it would stay until Mr Grierson was summoned.

Through the door she heard a sudden burst of high-pitched, hysterical laughter. Almost knocking Alison over in her attempts to accost the criminal, she rushed to the door and fell flat, tripping over the huddle of tin cars. There was nothing to see except the black tarmac path, with its lavender bushes on each side, and the slender rowan saplings near the door, but these, she noticed, had been trampled flat, and several of them pulled up by the roots.

The terrified woman picked herself up and dusted herself down a little. In the trees, fainter now, the awful lunatic laughter went on and on. Aunt Phyllis marched inside, shut the door, and locked it. Who on earth could have done all this? Someone with muscle, obviously, someone strong enough to heave that stone with great force through a window and to tear up those sturdy saplings, roots and all. And yet, it had sounded like a *woman's* voice…

Whoever it was needed medical help, she decided. Or could it be somebody from a local gang in Kirkmichael, a gang with a grudge against Grierson? She knew he wasn't popular round here.

She washed Alison's hands and face and walked boldly through the main house and up the grand stairway. When she knocked on the door of Grierson's suite David Blakeman himself answered it, brushes in hand. Aunt Phyllis swayed as she spoke. She really *was* getting a migraine. Her head was starting to sing, and she had the familiar spots before her eyes.

"Migraine," she blurted out. "I'll have to lie down in my room. Can you take her? And – er – someone's broken a window in the basement. I think Mr Grierson ought to come down later, and I'll explain what's happened."

David Blakeman was covered with paint. Grierson wasn't going to take kindly to Alison cavorting about in the studio. Well, he'd just have to unbend a little, and put up with it. Phyllis certainly looked most unwell, and there was a queer, startled look in those wide-awake blue eyes of hers, a look he'd never seen before. She was a person who always kept herself under strict control.

Halfway down the stairs again she remembered the dough. She must restore it to its pan before going to bed, otherwise there'd be no bread at all that day.

Back in the kitchen she rescued the dusty lump from behind the door, brushed it down, removed a few hairs and put it back on the stove. Then she swept the floor free of glass and gravel and put the dustpan and its contents next to the big white stone. This was evidence too. Mr Grierson might ask all kinds of awkward questions, and she must be sure of her facts. A pity Oliver hadn't been with her. He'd tell the man *precisely* what had happened.

It was still cold in the kitchen. Aunt Phyllis emptied the remains of the stewed tea into a cup and swallowed it down. It didn't warm her at all, she'd got a real attack of the shakes and shivers. A hot water bottle was the only answer.

Bowed almost in half, like an old, old woman, she crept about, opening cupboards, looking for one, and all the time that terrible screeching laughter rang round and round in her aching brain. She simply couldn't get the devilish noise out of her head.

CHAPTER NINE

Colin kept his binoculars trained on the old man, but not for long. A haze was coming down, between the island and the shore, shimmering strands of it, spreading out across the water like wreaths of fine grey gauze. The boat had disappeared into the mist in an eerie silence and Colin was left on the shingle, wondering how on earth they were going to get back, calculating whether he could swim across.

He turned round and made for the castle. Unless the others brought it up he wasn't going to discuss the problem of their return trip, not yet anyway. They were here, it was beautiful. Surely no one would be mean enough just to leave them there, not unless the old man was a real nutter? Perhaps he was a tramp who'd got himself on to the Lagg estate, to make a bit of money on the sly. Who on earth could it be, though? On the boat Oliver had whispered something about the National Trust for Scotland. That was a laugh, their guides were impeccably turned out, like Park Rangers. They didn't wear filthy old plaids and they didn't look about a hundred years old either.

It was a tiny island but, to start with, they all went exploring on their own. On the small patch of bright green grass she'd seen from the mainland, Prill caught sight of a goat nibbling away at the luxuriant long grass. So someone inhabited this minute island, at least in the summer. She must keep her eyes skinned and find out what they used for living quarters. But first she'd have a closer look at that goat.

"Stay girl, *stay*," she ordered Jessie, off the leash now they were on dry land again. But the dog took no notice and tore after her, yelping and leaping about with such noisy high spirits that the goat took fright and disappeared round the corner of the crumbling tower. Prill scrambled after it over heaps of fallen masonry, but the creature had gone.

She stared across the grass to the loch, and beyond it to the spread of low grey hills, perfectly reflected in the glassy waters. It felt right here, in spite of that foul old boatman. She wondered whether, years ago, it had been a place of sanctuary for someone, or simply a place where holy men came, to busy themselves only with God.

Prill was romantic. The mood of the place stole upon her like music as she stood there, enjoying the small breeze on her face. Jessie, having scared away the goat, now stood quite peacefully by her side. The girl patted her. It was as if all the gloomy things were back on the shore, in Lagg Castle and its woodlands. There was only peace here.

She found Colin inside the squat square tower,

climbing about amongst the rubble. The place had no roof and ivy was clawing up at the inside walls like a thick green arm.

"It's very picturesque," he said, as she came in under the low, round doorway, "but I wouldn't give it much longer unless someone comes and shores it up. What a mess. That ivy ought to come off, for a start. It's destroying the stonework."

The floor of the tower was heaped with building equipment. There was a rusty concrete mixer, ladders, and piles of planks. In one corner scaffolding had been constructed but it only went up about ten feet. "This is typical of Mr Grierson," Colin said, "according to Duncan, a year or so ago he decided Hag's Folly could become a tourist attraction, so he got this lot brought over on a boat. It must have taken some doing. Look at all that timber, just left to rot."

"Why didn't he go through with it?"

"Oh, he applied for a grant to pay for it all, but they wouldn't give him as much as he wanted, and he fell out with them. So the builders were sent away while it was all sorted out. Don't suppose they'll ever come back. He's so mean."

"That's why he got Dad to paint him," Prill said fiercely. "He's a millionaire, according to Granny MacCann. He could be done by somebody really famous, but that'd cost thousands, whereas Dad's still struggling, and doesn't ask great fees. He's a *horrible* man."

"It'll be a good picture though," Colin said loyally. "Unless Dad gives up before it's finished. They've already had a few disagreements."

"He does make money from this place, you know," Prill murmured, her mind still on Grierson's millions. "He sometimes lets it for the summer. People camp here. And Duncan rows trippers across too, in July and August. Aunt Phyllis said that'd be a nice little job for one of us, something that'd—"

"Don't say it, *keep us out of trouble*. She seems to think we're worse than The Bash Street Kids."

"Where's Oliver?" Prill said, suddenly missing him. He wasn't allowed to read comics, or watch TV.

"He's in the dungeon, if you can call it one. Come and have a look. Hold your nose, though, it stinks."

The dungeon was a small square cell at the bottom of a twisting stairway. Oliver was in there, on his hands and knees, going over the floor painstakingly with a torch. Prill and Colin stood on the steps and watched.

"It's no good," he said, over his shoulder. "Some silly fool's concreted it over. You'd need a pickaxe to get this lot up. I bet it was Mr Grierson."

"Perhaps he murdered his wife and put her here under the cold, cold stones," said Colin. "Can you imagine him, rowing across at dead of night, with her body in a sack?"

Prill giggled.

"She died in a riding accident actually," Oliver

79

reminded them in a cold little voice. "I told you that."

"Why do you want to get the floor up, Oliver?" Prill asked. He was a great digger, and finder of treasures, but a solid concrete floor must surely defeat even him.

"Oh, I just thought it might be interesting," he said evasively. "There might be all kinds of stuff under here, especially if the archaeologists haven't had first pick, and according to the pamphlet this place has never been excavated properly."

"So you're not trying to find the tunnel, then?" hinted Colin. He was sure Oliver *was* and that he'd found the story in his little guide. But just for once he found he was telling his cousin something he didn't know.

"It's a local legend," Colin explained. "Centuries ago the great lord's chief piper offended him or something, and he was thrown into a dungeon under this castle. The idea was to starve him to death, and he knew it. But he also knew that a tunnel was supposed to lead out of the dungeons, right under the loch, and come out somewhere on the slopes of one of those hills. The Hill of Doon it's called, the highest of them."

"Where did you hear this?" Oliver said suspiciously. It wasn't like Colin, he was more interested in sport than the finer points of archaeology, which was why they didn't really get on.

"From Duncan. He always tells that story to the trippers when he brings them over in his boat. Anyway, you've not heard the best bit yet. *Listen*. Somehow he did find the tunnel, and got into it."

"How?"

"Oh, I don't know. Don't spoil it, Oll. He got into this tunnel and tried to make his escape, under the loch, to freedom. But he got lost, and years later someone went down there and found a pile of bones and the remains of the bagpipes on top of them."

"Why didn't—"

"And... *and*..." Colin said darkly, "to this very day, at certain times of of the year, you're supposed to be able to hear the poor man's ghostly bagpipe music drifting up through the water."

Prill was far away. She could see that poor man, stumbling about helplessly in pitch darkness, in a rat-infested tunnel. She could see the harsh-faced lord sitting on his throne, nursing his wrath, she could hear the sad-sweet music of the pipes.

"I *hate* bagpipes," Oliver said coolly, getting up from his knees and snapping his torch off. "There are lots of stories like that. You really can't take them seriously, you know. What just might have a grain of truth in it is the idea of the tunnel. I mean, if people *had* been imprisoned here, for years and years that is, they might start digging a way out, in their desperation. They did it in the prison camps, during the war."

"I'm hungry," said Colin, ignoring all this. So much for Duncan's wonderful story. It was typical of Oliver to pour cold water on it. He was always after the actual facts and figures. There wasn't much romance in his soul. "Come on," he said tetchily. "Forget it, Oll. It's only a story. Where did you leave the rucksack? I could eat a horse."

"If we *did* do any excavating," Oliver said slowly, "we'd need some air freshener or something. It absolutely stinks down here. An animal must have died in it."

It smelt quite sweet to Prill. She couldn't understand what the boys were going on about. To her the smell was grass and fields, and an animal's warm breath. It was a familiar smell. Jessie had leaped into the dark little hole and was nosing about in the corners.

"Come on, girl," Prill shouted, as the boys scrambled past her, up the steps. "Dinner time. Come *on*."

But the dog was whimpering and sniffing about busily. Something down there had interested her. It was as though she was being dragged away from her favourite friend. "Bye bye, Jessie," Prill said firmly. These were the only words that would bring the dog when she was being really disobedient.

She turned and began to climb up the twisting steps. Then she looked back. There, at the bottom, a figure was standing quite still and looking straight at her, the tallish figure of a young woman. She had soft brown hair and a pale brown skin with a large mole on the left cheek. A dark green cloak was clutched tightly round her with one hand. The other held the goat she'd seen, on a bit of rope.

Prill fled. Clutching at the powdery walls for some kind of support, she stumbled up the rotting steps, across the littered courtyard, and out under the round doorway. Just once she turned back, and summoned the dog, but Jessie seemed riveted to the top of the steps. She was yelping and fawning, and making her growly friendly noise. At nothing.

Aunt Phyllis's picnic was a good one but the boys ate Prill's share. She couldn't swallow. Why, oh why, had she run away? She sat silently on the grass, staring out across the loch with that figure etched on her memory. The goat on the string, the brown mole, the large pale arm coming out from under the rags, to keep the dusty green cloak in place.

She was saying nothing, not yet. Prill had seen things before and had usually been laughed at. "Priscilla's a romantic, she's always seeing and hearing things beyond the ken of ordinary mortals," her father had said once, laughingly, to the owner of a holiday cottage they'd rented for the summer. And the landlady had said ruefully, "I'm interested in things like that too, dear. Trouble is, it's never people like us who actually *see* the ghost is it?" Now Prill had.

Colin rowed them back in a boat that looked

remarkably similar to the old man's. He'd found it half-hidden by scrubby bushes, on the other side of the little island.

"How can we?" Oliver said nervously. He was always very anxious about rules and regulations, and this might land them in trouble.

"Look," replied Colin, "he just went off and left us. That was hours ago. What are we supposed to do? He's not here. We've searched every inch of the place. Anyway, I doubt if it's the same boat. They all look alike to me. His is probably pulled up somewhere else, and we've missed it."

Colin was almost certain it *was* the same boat. What had happened to the ferryman was quite beyond him. He'd tell Duncan what had happened tonight. He'd know who the old man was, and if they ought to do anything about him.

They began to cross the water in an uneasy silence. "If we *did* hear the pipes," Oliver whispered, suddenly warming to Colin's story, "we could trace the line of that tunnel."

"Thought you said it was a load of old rubbish," Colin said rudely, sweating over the oars.

"Not quite. I think there's a grain of truth in it. Now why don't we get—"

"*Sh* Oll," Prill said suddenly. "There *is* a noise. Stop prattling, and listen."

They could hear a faint singing. It sounded as if it

was coming up through the water, a sweet rounded voice that Prill had heard before:

> "*Let not the errors of my youth,*
> *Or sins remembered be,*
> *In mercy for Thy goodness' sake,*
> *Oh Lord, remember me…*"

"It's a hymn," said Colin. "Someone's singing a hymn. Nice voice. One of the campers must have a radio on."

Prill said nothing. The field Mr Grierson rented out to campers was miles away, beyond the woods.

"It's a psalm actually," corrected Oliver, listening carefully. "It's Psalm 25, they sing it in church sometimes. It's a very old setting though."

Trust cleverclogs Oliver to know a thing like that, always parading his knowledge. He couldn't just be quiet and listen. Prill did, following the words, half fearing, half hoping that the woman she'd seen on the island might be here in the boat with them. But the voice was growing fainter now, drifting and dying like thin summer cloud. They were soon back on the shore and all helping to pull the boat up on to the shingle, knotting it tight to a rusty iron ring.

A terrible coldness clutched at Prill as she went back through the trees. The bracken had been scorched here too, all along the path.

"You know, someone really has got a grudge against

Mr Grierson," Colin said, "doing all this. It's so senseless. These woods'll go up in flames one day, if they don't sort him out. We'll have to tell Angus."

As the path twisted to the left, up a slope, a large hare bounded across the path. Colin immediately clapped his binoculars to his eyes. "What a whopper," he whispered, "and it's not a bit frightened of us either, look." The hare had stopped in the middle of the path. It was enormous, a silky-sandy colour with a splash of white on its back. "We ought to tell Duncan. He goes shooting with his father sometimes. It'd made a good pie. Look at its great belly."

The hare certainly looked sleek and well-fed, like a household pet or something from a zoo. Prill expected Jessie to go straight for it, but she didn't. She backed away and whimpered, and buried her nose in the girl's skirt.

Prill patted her. She saw nothing very clearly yet, but she believed that something very strange had just happened to them. They'd been *tricked* into going across to the island, and it was the old man's firm intention to leave them there. Colin could interrogate the Rosses all he liked but he wouldn't get anywhere. She was certain that they would never see that strange, hunched figure ever again.

And someone had been with them at Hag's Folly. Prill knew that even before she'd seen the silent figure at the bottom of the steps. It was someone Jessie liked, and something to do with the singing and with the sweet animal smell that kept wafting to her on the quiet breeze.

It wasn't here, though, not in these dark woods. Here there was only a strange bloated hare, and blackened trees, and coldness, coldness all around.

Oliver had gone so far ahead of them he was almost out of sight. He'd spotted some old books in an outhouse that morning, a couple of dusty bundles tied up, ready for the dump, and he'd decided he'd better go through them. Kirkmichael was only a small place and it didn't have a library, and there was no way he could get into Dumfries.

Hares... there was something about them, but he just couldn't remember what. They were magic, or evil, or something. A book on witchcraft would tell him a thing like that, if he was lucky enough to find one. Grierson had enough books. Perhaps he'd have to sneak up to his library one night, and poke around...

The man on the loch was quite a different matter. Oliver was rather pleased with himself there. He'd acted well, asking Colin all those silly questions about park rangers, and pretending to worry about the boat. If he was right about Aggie Ross, she could assume any shape she wanted, an animal, a tree, an invisible whisper on the wind – or a weather-beaten old man with skeleton hands.

But he wasn't telling the others what he thought, not

yet. They hadn't really believed him last night. He needed more evidence. She'd have to show herself again. So they could only wait for her next move. Like innocents trapped in some devilish game.

CHAPTER TEN

Aunt Phyllis's home-made tea was not a brilliant success. Mr Blakeman had argued with Grierson, who'd wanted a tray brought up to them so they could have another session on the painting.

"That man!" he muttered, grabbing a slice of bread. "He's obsessed. He thinks he owns people. I'm beginning to feel like a prisoner in that damned studio."

Aunt Phyllis frowned and watched everyone eat. She didn't approve of swear words, nor did she like the way David Blakeman gobbled his food. It was a quick way to indigestion and stomach ulcers.

Dad always ate like that when something had irritated him. He soon slowed down, though, when he tasted the bread. So did everybody else, and Alison wailed and flung her bit across the room. The loaf looked wholesome enough, but there was definitely something wrong with it. It had such a strong irony taste. "Almost like licking your finger when it's been bleeding," Prill whispered to Colin.

"Eat up," Mr Blakeman mumbled, overhearing. "It won't kill us. We mustn't offend your aunt. She's being such a trooper, doing all this cooking."

All the same, they could have done without all the

muck. Everyone was surreptitiously removing strands of hair and bits of grit from their mouths, and dropping them under the table. Aunt Phyllis got her share too, and felt secretly embarrassed. It must have happened when the dough fell on the floor, though that couldn't account for the strange taste. She baked her own bread week in, week out, at home, but she'd never made a loaf like this before. Could it be the local water? She just might have to give in, and order some from that baker.

"I'm going on a diet if she makes any more like this," Colin muttered in Prill's ear. "It's uneatable. Thought she was supposed to be a *good* cook. I'd rather have Mother's Pride."

Prill didn't answer. She struggled with the unchewable bread and thought, "Blood. It tastes of blood." and she thought of her aunt's trials with the stove, and how she'd reported Alison to her father for blowing it out. Aunt Phyllis had forgotten the limitations of a two-year-old, if she'd ever known them. Alison wasn't up to a trick like that.

Something at Lagg was getting at them. It was a bit like a fairy tale where a little imp keeps blowing all the candles out, and turning the milk sour. But Prill was beginning to suspect that it was much more, something to do with the history of the place, and with Hugo Grierson. Perhaps Oliver's wild theory was nearer the truth than she and Colin would admit. It certainly felt as if their very coming here had roused some evil, sleeping thing to life again. Something from deep in the past, something to torment them – *and* Hugo Grierson. Could it really have started with an old heap of stones?

And what about the singing? At least they'd all heard it, out on the loch. Prill knew that it was the same voice she'd heard, in the middle of the night, and that it was something to do with that hand at the window, and the sweet country smell, and that all of it was good. There wasn't a trace of malice in the face she'd seen on the island. It just didn't fit in with Oliver's notion of a witch at large.

There was malice here. Spite and mockery were all around them at Lagg. It was in the broken window and the very food they were eating. It was as if an invisible war was going on between something essentially good and something desperately wicked, with the Blakemans and poor Aunt Phyllis caught in the middle.

Oliver was the cleverest of them all, and he knew something strange was afoot. Prill decided to choose her moment and tell him everything, tonight perhaps, when they'd been up to see the Rosses. Duncan's father had invited them for "a bite and a wee sup". Ramshaws was the most desolate cottage imaginable but it was better than having to stay at Lagg Castle all evening.

They were just setting off when Grierson marched into the kitchen to inspect the broken window. He was really rude to Aunt Phyllis. She had her explanation all prepared, how first the gravel had come in, and how she'd dashed outside, and then there'd been this really terrible crash. But Grierson clearly didn't want to know. He cut her off in mid-sentence, muttering darkly about "village thugs" and "sheer mindless vandalism", running a steel tape round the window frame and jotting measurements down in a notebook. "I'll tell Ross tomorrow," he said. "This is a little job for him."

"We can tell him for you," Oliver offered, chirpily, from the doorway. "We're going up there now."

"Why?" barked Grierson. "What for? That man's got his work to do. I don't pay him for doing nothing."

Well, you hardly *do* pay him, Colin was thinking, and anyway, his evenings are his own. What's it got to do with you?

"Duncan's invited us," Prill said very sweetly. "To – to show us his things. And they're giving us supper." Her large brown eyes looked straight into his piggy little blue ones. Stop us if you dare, she was saying. "Come on, you two," she shouted, already outside on the path.

"I – you won't find them in," Grierson called after them, with that nasty thin twist in his voice. "It's a hard climb up to Ramshaws, and it'll be a waste of effort. Ross plays bingo on Wednesdays, in the hall at Kirkmichael. The boy goes with him."

"Well, he definitely said tonight," Oliver announced firmly. "So I expect they're skipping it for once."

"We can go, can't we, Aunt Phyllis?" Colin said. She was frowning and looking slightly bewildered. Mr

Grierson clearly wanted to stop them. But she'd heard Angus Ross issue the invitation herself. So what was all this about bingo?

"Yes, yes," she said, "off you go. I think, Mr Grierson," she continued, turning back to him, but she could have saved her breath. He'd stormed out of the kitchen and shut the door with an almighty slam.

"There'll be more broken windows if he carries on like that," she said tartly as his footsteps died away, gathering up all the uneaten bread and butter and wondering if it would make some kind of pudding.

To get to Ramshaws they set off as for Granny MacCann's but turned left down the main road instead of crossing over into the woods. Carlin's Crag was very close here, and the route took them right under the overhang.

"Ugh," said Prill, quickening her pace, "it gives me the creeps. It's… it's like a face. Hurry up Colin."

He'd stopped, and was staring up at it, his arms folded. "You know, it'd be marvellous to climb," he said. "Why don't we?"

"Because we've got no time," snapped Oliver, looking at his watch. "We've got to be back by nine and it's nearly six-thirty already."

"I don't mean now. I just mean on one of the days. I bet Duncan's been up it."

"I bet he's not," snorted Oliver. "Look at all that

barbed wire. It's out of bounds. It's *dangerous*. You'd need ropes and hooks and all kinds of stuff to get up there. People have been killed on that crag, Ma told me." They'd never get him up there, not ever. Oliver was terrified of heights.

"It's still the quickest way to Ramshaws," Colin said longingly. He loved rock scrambles, the worse the better. "Look, you can see the smoke from their chimney. *Bingo in Kirkmichael*. That man can't even tell a good lie."

Opposite the Crag was a small field full of tents. Some boys in bright anoraks were standing round a barbecue, poking a fire into life with sticks. "D'you want a hot dog?" one of them called out. "We've got plenty."

"Yes, come over and join us," shouted somebody's father. "You're from the big house, aren't you?"

"We can't, not tonight," Colin said. "But we'll come another day, thanks."

It was a very orderly campsite with all the tents arranged in neat rows, exactly according to Grierson's rules. They didn't seem the kind of boys who'd go mad with matches in a forest. Prill noticed another rule, too, on the gate. "*No transistor radios to be played on this site.*" That was something else to explain to Oliver, when she told him about the singing.

They rounded the bottom of the Crag and found the steep back road that went up to Ramshaws. Parked at the bottom was an ancient Ford van.

"That's what Angus has to use for going round all

Mr Grierson's properties," said Colin. "It's about twenty years old and I should think the bottom's about to drop out of it." Grierson himself drove a Mercedes, and there was also a brand new Range Rover in the huge triple garage under the house.

"What do you expect?" said Oliver. "He *wants* to drive the Rosses away. Angus is always getting stranded miles from home, in that van. My mother told me."

It was a long, hard pull up to the cottage. Nobody hurried, they were all too short of breath, but the slow climb gave them a chance to look at Lagg's woodlands properly for once, and to see how neglected they were. They saw rotten wood all over the place, where trees had fallen and been left to decay, great bare patches where fires had eaten into the plantings and the saplings not been replaced, outlines of broad woodland rides with grass and rotting timbers, and moss growing over them. Grierson needed a small army of men to clean up his forest but all he had was Angus Ross.

He was a very silent individual, a bigger version of Duncan but with lank, dark hair instead of his son's ginger curls. He ladled out stew from a big iron pot and the children were given hunks of coarse brown bread to eat it with.

"It's good," he grunted, "A made it masel," as he saw Prill hesitate. After Aunt Phyllis's loaf she wasn't sure she could touch bread for a while. The stew was tasty though; rabbit, thickened with big chunks of vegetable. Colin liked the herby taste. " 'Tis Grierson's rabbit," Angus explained with a wry smile. "Dinna let it poison ye noo."

"It's great," Colin said enthusiastically. Aunt Phyllis's tea had been inedible, and he was hollow. "We saw an enormous hare today, as we were coming up from the loch," he said, with his mouth full. "It was gigantic. You couldn't miss it either. It had a big splash of white on its back."

Duncan was interested at once. Bagging a really fine hare would be quite something, if only he could persuade his father to let him use the big gun. He was only half-listening to their questions about the old man who'd abandoned them so abruptly at Hag's Folly.

Angus wasn't listening either, hunched over the miserable fire. "Will you look at that!" he grumbled, "Bits o' sticks! Ye canna keep a good fire burning wi'kindlers. This hoos is so damp you could wring it oot like a sponge. D'you wonder the boy coughed from Christmas tae Easter? Aye, an' the good logs A've pulled from the hill piled high down the yard, an' still A'm left wi' no' but the brashings tae burn, unless A doff ma bonnet an' pay auld Hughie for a load. Och he's tight, that yin, always thinkin' o' ways tae claw back ma pay. Not that it's ower much tae start with." He spat into the snivelling flames.

"Er, the old man," Colin said warily, embarrassed at

the man's bitter burst of rage. "Any idea who it might have been? Are there tramps around, do you know, people sleeping rough?"

Angus shook his head. "A've no' seen travellin' folk hereabouts for a good wee while. But A'll row across the morn's morn, and sneak a look for ye. Yon Grierson'd no' like anybody but his-sel makin' money frae the estate."

"It was a really mean trick, just going off like that," Colin said defiantly. Prill and Oliver made no comment. They exchanged furtive glances, then stared at the floor.

Prill looked frightened. She *knows*, Oliver said to himself, his heart thudding nervously against his ribs. Her brother may still think I'm potty but Prill *knows*.

CHAPTER ELEVEN

After the meal there was an awkward silence. The hissing fire didn't begin to heat the damp cottage, and the children grew cold and bored. Angus was still staring moodily into the ashes, poking them about with a stick, and carrying on his dreary monologue about Hugo Grierson.

"It's small help we can be tae oursels," he complained. "We're no' even permitted tae have a few hens runnin' aboot the place, for a good fresh egg, without Hughie Grierson complainin'. Can't abide the scrawk of a cock in the morn, he tel't me, stupid auld fuil! All these silly wee things he does, just tae annoy. It's more like he canna abide tae see onie man more content than his-sel. Aye, he couldna be more miserable in hell itself." He suddenly brought his fist crashing down on the bare table, making all the soup dishes rattle.

There was no mention at all of his absent wife. According to Granny MacCann she was "a wicket dally-doll" who'd run off years ago, with someone who lived "in a big way", beyond Dumfries.

There was the most terrible loathing in Angus Ross's face. They'd only seen hate like that in one other person, Grierson of Lagg. The man obviously blamed him for all the troubles of his life, even the ones he'd had nothing at all to do with, like the wife running off.

Someone had to make conversation. "We went down to the beach," Prill started nervously. "We were interested in the old memorial."

"Och, aye," muttered Angus, his shoulders stiffening, over the fire. A pronounced silence followed.

"What's it there for?" demanded Oliver abruptly. He was beginning to feel irritated by Angus Ross – he was hardly any better than Grierson. He just grunted at you, like a pig. "It's a Ross memorial, isn't it? Well, that's what Mr Grierson said." (Or was that a lie too, like the bingo?)

Angus didn't answer. Oliver persisted. "Don't you know *anything* about it, nothing at all?"

"Folk roond here dinna say much aboot it," the man said, through gritted teeth. "It marks the scene of a death. Is that good enough for ye?"

"But Mr Grierson said you looked after it," whispered Colin. He was getting rather nervous. Although hardly a word had been exchanged the atmosphere in the cottage was becoming thick and explosive.

"There are plenty o' Rosses roond Galloway," Duncan cut in hurriedly, glancing at his father. "But we're the nearmaist. And it's a Ross memorial. When the wood rots we'll mek a new yin."

"In case folk forget," added Angus darkly.

"How often?" said Oliver. "How often is the wood replaced?"

"The last time A was only a wee'n, forty years, mebbe mair. This ane should last another ten. But it must be watched man, *watched*. Grierson might tak an axe tae it, or faggots…"

"So what exactly happened there?" said Oliver. "And who's Aggie Ross? Granny MacCann mentioned her." He introduced the name as casually as possible, but the effect was electric.

Angus glared at Duncan, obviously telling him to keep his mouth shut, then took up his charred stick again and poked quite violently at the dying fire.

"Aggie Ross? *Aggie Ross?*" he repeated savagely. "She's *nocht* tae do wi' us. Ye shouldna listen tae an auld wumman's bletherin'."

"What about the memorial then?" Oliver said stoutly. He didn't give up easily and he knew perfectly well that Angus was lying. He obviously knew quite a bit about Aggie Ross.

There was a silence, then the man said harshly, "A've tel't ye already, someone died there once."

Oliver's mouth was framing another question but Colin gave him a hefty kick under the table. The man's face was quite alarming; it was black, as black and murderous as that awful portrait, halfway up the stairs at Lagg Castle.

Nobody asked any more questions, Angus was

eventually persuaded to take down his best shotgun and show it to them, and Duncan dropped big hints about going after that hare. Before they set off for Lagg they were shown Angus's prize possession, a polished silver bullet in a little glass case.

"See the date," he said proudly. "1730 this was made, in Dumfries, tae kill th'auld witch finder, Grierson of Lagg. A siller bullet was usually kep' for the de'il himsel. Aye, 'twas the only thing that would kill a carlin an a'."

"A *what*?" said Prill.

"A *witch*," translated Oliver. "Carlin's Crag, it means *Witch's* Crag. I told you before!" What he was dying to ask, but didn't dare, was whether that stake in the sand had anything to do with Aggie Ross.

Angus was turning the polished bullet over in his hand, and his thoughts were clearly wandering. "Tis a pity it didna do its work," he said, more to himself than to the three children. "Tis a pity th'auld witch finder man wasna murdered in his bed, then the line would ha' died oot lang syne."

Then Grierson at the Big House would never have been born, was his obvious, unspoken thought.

They were later than they should have been getting back. Angus lent them an oil lantern but they didn't really need it; it was a fine evening with a large clear moon. All along the path, thick shadows lay on the bushes like black cloths hung out to dry. A wind was getting up, and the rustling forest was spooky.

They kept closer together on the steep track and hurried down towards the road, singing daft songs to keep their spirits up. Nobody liked this part of the walk very much. Next time they must definitely come home in daylight. None of them saw the shadows shift and move or something detach itself from the low bushes and come drifting down after them, like cloud, its low moaning laugh drowned by the rising wind.

Aunt Phyllis was looking out for them anxiously, and she bundled them straight off to bed. Mr Grierson had taken Dad into Kirkmichael, for dinner at its one good hotel.

"Was he feeling all right?" asked Colin sarcastically. "Treating someone to a meal?"

His aunt sniffed. "Guilty, I'd say. Making up for that nasty temper. There's just no knowing what goes on inside that head of his. He blows hot one minute, cold the next. I've never met anyone like him."

"*You* were the one he was rude to," Oliver said loyally. "*You* should have gone out to dinner."

"*Me?*" Aunt Phyllis was aghast at the very idea of eating and drinking with Hugo Grierson. "No, thank you very much. Anyway, someone had to stay with Alison. I've been quite comfortable. Now, go and undress all of you. Clean those teeth and no reading. It's late."

On his way to bed Colin asked her for a couple of

aspirins. "I've got a headache," he told her. "I won't get to sleep if I don't take something." She was immediately very interested, and began to quiz him. When did it start and how bad was it, and had he any other symptoms? Aches and pains were the very business of life to Auntie Phyllis. No wonder Oliver was so interested in his own.

"It's just a bit of a headache," Colin said cautiously. It wasn't, it was one of the worst pains he'd ever had and it had come quite suddenly. But he didn't want the Spanish Inquisition from his aunt. The pounding sensation in his head was horribly sharp, but it came and went. It wasn't a dull ache, more like a series of blows, as if someone had a little hammer and was systematically driving tacks into his skull.

His aunt was watching him very carefully as he swallowed the pills. He looked robust and healthy enough, and he certainly didn't have a temperature. She hoped it wasn't the start of the awful Blakeman flu bug; that had begun with headaches.

Prill was in for a bad night too. She kept herself awake till the whole house was quiet, then she slipped out of bed and crept along to Oliver's room. She knew perfectly well that he regularly disobeyed his mother, and read by the light of a torch. This time he'd not even switched his lamp off. There was a thin yellow line under the door.

"Oll," she whispered. "*Oll*, it's me, Prill. Can I come in? I want to talk to you."

There were little shuffling noises and Oliver appeared in the doorway, wrapped in his counterpane. Prill was all muffled up too, in her dressing gown. The basement did get very cold at night.

He let her in with his finger pressed dramatically against his lips. Aunt Phyllis was snoring peacefully, right next door. "*Sh*," he said sharply, the minute she opened her mouth. "You'll have to hurry up. She's a very light sleeper."

It wasn't a very good beginning. Oliver seemed rather on edge, probably because Prill had interrupted something important. His bed was littered with books and papers, several of them covered with his thin, spindly writing.

She sat on the floor and tried to explain calmly about what she'd seen and heard last night. She told him everything she could remember but it obviously came out all wrong. Oliver seemed confused and kept interrupting.

"What woman?" he broke in sharply. "What did she look like? What hymns? I don't follow…" and, "So what if the old man *did* go off and leave us? Colin thinks he's just some sort of nut-case."

"But you don't, do you, Oll?"

"No, I don't. I think it was *her*, not your woman, the *witch*."

He couldn't think straight. He sat on the bed in silence, staring into space. Prill had arrived at the wrong moment with her story of voices in the night and of a ghost on Hag's Island. He'd been doing some reading, and she'd knocked just as he'd reached the important part. He didn't like being interrupted in the middle of his researches, he liked to present his case to people all cut and dried.

Besides, what she'd just told him made everything much more complicated.

"There *was* something very special about her, Oll," Prill was saying passionately. "I can't really explain it… a stillness, a sense of holiness, almost." She said the last bit very quietly, with obvious embarrassment. "You do believe me, don't you?"

"Of course I do," he said, but he sounded grumpy. He was thinking very hard. This new development had knocked all his theories about witches and Aggie Ross sideways. How could a saintly character, who went round singing hymns all the time, have anything to do with a demon like her? It *must* be a local character, someone who lived in a cottage somewhere and wandered about doing slightly odd things, someone a bit simple.

He was busily bundling all his papers together so Prill couldn't see what he'd been doing, but the title of one of the books caught her eye before he whipped it smartly under his pillow. It was called *Witches in Tartan – A Study of the Black Art in Scotland*.

CHAPTER TWELVE

"You *know* what's going on, don't you, Oll?" Prill said, pulling the book out, and looking at it. The boy snatched it back and shoved it under the pillow again.

"Why do that, for heaven's sake? I was only—"

"*Shh…* it's *her*," he whispered frantically, pointing in the direction of the snoring. "She hates anything like this, it's against what she believes, she calls it dabbling. If she knew I was reading a book about witches she's kill me."

"Why *are* you reading it?" asked Prill, an unpleasant chill creeping over her suddenly.

"Because we're being haunted, of course," the boy replied, maddeningly matter of fact, as if he was talking about the weather, "and we've got to find out all we can! There's obviously something wrong here. I knew it the minute we moved the stones at Lochashiel, and when you noticed all those scorched bushes."

"But, Oll, why didn't you *say* something? I knew too." On a sudden impulse Prill took his thin little hand, and squeezed it. "It's better to share. Why be so secretive about everything?"

"I was afraid you might laugh," Oliver muttered, in a very small voice.

"I thought you'd laugh at *me*," admitted Prill, "but, Oll, I didn't imagine that woman on Hag's Island. She *was* there. With the goat. But... oh, I don't understand. She's *good*, Oll. She's not doing all these creepy things."

"Hang on," he interrupted. "You may as well read this. It's not much to go on, but it's all I could find. There are some mouldy old books tied up in an outhouse. It was all in there."

Prill took the sheet of paper he held out to her. She read, "Facts about witches, 1 to 5. 1 : Witches cannot cross running water. (Note – this would be why the ferryman skirted the burn, where it makes a current in the loch.) 2 : Witches make wax or cloth images of their chosen victims and drive nails into their skulls, to cause splitting headaches, sometimes resulting in death. 3 : Witches scorch the ground they tread on, turning the soil barren. 4 : The rowan tree wards off evil and is planted outside a house to try and keep the witch away. 5 : If disturbed, witches become violent and copy the actions of poltergeists (restless spirits who plague the living)."

Prill read it carefully, twice, shuddered, and handed it back.

"Who *is* she Oll?" she whispered. "And why is she after *us*?"

"I don't know," he muttered, folding up the paper and hiding it inside *Witches in Tartan*.

He wasn't going to tell her everything. Not yet anyway. He knew that they ought to take all those stones they'd moved back to Lochashiel. He might convince Prill of his theory if he actually showed her what he'd found there, in the mud. On the other hand, she might pass out too.

Prill's dreams were terrible that night. She saw the pale arm again, just outside the window, and she saw a pale hand tapping, gently at first then becoming more and more insistent, as if the woman was desperate to come in. The singing was desperate too, there was no sweetness in it, no content:

> *"In judgement therefore shall not stand*
> *Such as ungodly are;*
> *Nor in the assembly of the just*
> *Shall wicked men appear..."*

The voice was harsh and the tune ragged, as if the singer was struggling to break free from some invisible tormentor.

At one point Prill sat bolt upright, convinced that she was wide awake. In the room, only inches from her face, was a dark shadow, not wispy and insubstantial but heavy and thick, like coarse cloth. It was coming straight for her, towering up over the bed. The force of it was driving her back on to the pillows and it was grappling with her hands, twisting them together cruelly, behind her back...

She screamed aloud. Her door was suddenly pushed open and the ugly shadow withered and shrank to the shape of her dark red dressing gown, swinging on its hook. Colin was standing just outside, in the passage, with a bottle of pills in his hand.

"Are you OK?" he said sleepily. "I heard a noise. You cried out."

Now she was actually awake Prill felt sick with relief. "Yes, yes," she muttered. "I must have been dreaming. I – what's wrong with *you* though? Where've you been?"

"Only to the bathroom. I've got a splitting headache. Aunt Phyllis gave me some aspirin at bedtime, but I'll have to have another one.

"You *look* OK," Prill pointed out. The familiar freckled face and mop of ginger hair comforted her. She didn't want him to go. "Perhaps it's the cold," she said. "That can give you a headache. It's like a fridge in this place at night."

Colin shrugged. "Well, I'm not staying here freezing to death. I just hope I've not got Mum's bug. Don't tell her by the way, if you write. She'll think it's a brain tumour."

All he wanted was to lie flat and wait for sleep to come, but his head was full of hammers, all dinning away at one exquisitely tender spot. It was unbearable.

He had restless, pain-filled dreams, all about Hag's Folly. They were rowing, endlessly rowing, across water the colour of black glass, water where the oars made no ripple or noise. The plaid had fallen right away from the old man's face, to reveal a fleshless skull, and the hand that snatched the money was all bone. Colin closed his eyes very tight lest the phantom rower should put coins on them, coins to pay the ferryman, on their journey to Death.

Oliver wasn't disturbed by bad dreams or headaches, and, having finished chapter six of *Witches in Tartan*, he settled down for a good night's sleep. But at about three o'clock a noise woke him, a terrific crash somewhere over his head, then the sound of breaking glass. Prill heard it too, and woke up for the second time, listening to the glass tinkling down on to some roof like the notes of a xylophone, then to a burst of crazy laughter, dying away into the heavy darkness.

Next morning it was horrible. They usually all had breakfast together, and it was a meal everyone enjoyed. But today Dad was missing, and Aunt Phyllis made them go straight up to Grierson's rooms without eating anything. Prill was still cleaning her teeth and Colin was pulling his trousers on when The Summons came.

The three children went panting up the back stairs. Since their official tour they'd been forbidden to use the main staircase. It hadn't pleased Colin. He was beginning to detest Hugo Grierson. He'd noticed how Duncan had to stay outside, like a dog, when Angus came up to the Big House, to get his orders for the day.

Mr Blakeman was waiting for them in the library. He looked extremely strained and tense, and he was fully occupied with Alison, who was tearing around pulling books off the shelves in great armfuls.

"Pretty," she babbled, as the shiny gilt and calf volumes tumbled to the floor in heaps. "Pretty books."

The scene in the library was anything but pretty. The room had been wrecked. The great windows that overlooked the forest and sea had been shattered, and huge gales were blowing through. The children, still only half-dressed, shivered and looked round. There was debris all over the floor, broken glass and splintered wood, pictures flung from the walls and trampled on in their frames, a rack of tobacco pipes hurled across the room and broken into pathetic fragments under a table. On top of this, an ugly leather-covered affair with bulbous legs and feet like lions' claws, were three huge stones, knobbled and white with green mossy stains on them, still powdered with earth. The whole room smelt of earth. Hugo Grierson stood with arms folded by the open door, resisting the temptation to deliver a stinging slap on Alison's bare legs, his thin, mean features set rock hard.

The three children stared in terrified silence. Grierson was mad. They were obviously going to be blamed for this somehow.

Prill's eyes crept upwards through the broken panes; she looked beyond the huge oak and the lawns and the woods to the endless sea, where the blackened stake, now half-submerged in the glittering tide, looked like the hulk of a long abandoned ship, or a great dark fin, for ever breaking the swirling golden water.

"It's not this I want you to see," snarled Grierson. "In *here*. Come on, in you go. I'm sure you'd like to see your father's handiwork in its early stages. Well, now you can."

They were half pushed, half dragged across the room, and through the studio door. Mr Blakeman did not intervene, but the atmosphere was electric. He was turning a slow dark pink colour, and he was clenching and unclenching his fists. In a minute he would erupt into one of his rare outbursts of pure rage. It was clear that Grierson was blaming everything on the children. The man was mad.

Colin, Prill and Oliver were not prepared for the sight in the studio. The high echoing room was empty apart from the painting gear, the big carved chair Grierson had posed in, and the canvas itself. Dad was a slow worker and there was little colour on the portrait as yet, but what he'd drawn in so far was Grierson to the life. Except that the whole thing had been monstrously defaced with thick paint.

On each side of the head, protruding ridiculously from the silky hair, were two gigantic ears, daubed on in bright red; a great drooping moustache had been painted in and from the now twisted and leering mouth came two great fangs, spotted with blood. The whole effect was devilish, though viewed another way the face was clown-like, making you want to laugh.

This Oliver did, out loud.

CHAPTER THIRTEEN

Mr Grierson went for him like a maniac and brought his hands down hard on the boy's puny shoulders. It was impossible to make out what he was saying, a white-hot anger was turning his speech into a series of such weird gobbling noises that they really thought he was going to have a fit.

"I'm sorry," the boy squeaked helplessly. "I didn't mean to laugh. It was just so unexpected… oh, oh I'm *sorry*…" and he went off into titters again.

The man really looked as though he was going to hit him. He raised his hand, and Oliver flinched away. There was an awful silence then Grierson flung the boy aside, like something filthy and disgusting. Oliver reeled, his glasses fell off and he tottered blindly across the studio floor. He'd stopped laughing and the tears had come into his eyes. It wasn't the pain, it was the unfairness of it all. He'd laughed out of sheer shock and embarrassment.

His uncle caught him and held him firmly, then the row started. All the time they were arguing, poor Oliver was held in front, like a hostage in a gun battle. Alison, alarmed at the raised voices, started to howl. Prill took her into her arms, feebly trying to distract her from the sight of Mr Grierson storming around the great barn of a room, shaking his fists at the portrait, then at Oliver, shouting and swearing at the top of his voice. Her father, vainly trying to control his temper, was shouting too now, as the deranged man's string of accusations grew wilder and wilder.

"*I've* heard you," he was screaming. "*I* know what you call this place. You call it Castle Dracula, don't you? And I suppose I'm the Count? Huh? *Huh?* I'm right, aren't I? Oh yes, I know what people say about me round here, the Rosses and the MacCanns, and all the rest of them, don't you worry. Well, I'll tell you something. Silly nicknames are one thing, but *this* is quite another!" He pointed at the ruined portrait with its pixie ears and its dripping fangs. "*This*," he repeated "*This*... well, it's the most tasteless joke I've ever seen in the whole of my life. You should be ashamed of yourselves, all of you, sneaking up here, wrecking my library, painting the—"

"*We had nothing to do with it*," a cold angry voice interrupted. "How dare you accuse us of this? What sort of people do you think we are?" It wasn't Mr Blakeman who spoke, it was Colin. He'd walked right up to Grierson and he now stood solidly in front of him, like a boxer squaring up for a fight. He felt like turning that hard, arrogant face into a red pulp.

"Colin!" his father warned, but the boy took no notice. "The idea of any of us heaving stones through your windows is absolutely ridiculous for a start!" he yelled. "We'd need to be sixty feet tall, for one thing, and look at them, I couldn't lift any of them, let alone throw one through a window. Anyway, why on earth *should* we? And why would we ruin Dad's painting? All right, we *do* call it Castle Dracula, but it's only a joke. We think it's lovely here... Why should we want to spoil anything? How could you even dream of such a thing? I think it's terrible of you."

"Sit down, Colin," Mr Blakeman said very quietly, pushing a stool under him. To everyone's astonishment the boy had started to cry, and there was now an awkward silence in the room, apart from his sniffling.

Colin hated himself, but he couldn't help it. There had been something terrifying about the sight of Hugo Grierson, ugly as sin in his wild, uncontrollable rage. He was the snake in this Paradise, surrounded by beauty but eaten up by hatred. Watching him in his anger, Colin had seen Grierson turn into someone else. He'd no longer looked the elegant modern man but like that portrait on the stairs, Lagg, the black-bearded witch-finder. Even as he wiped his eyes with his sleeve, Colin sensed that if only they could find out what had happened at Lagg in the past they might understand a lot more about its present owner. It was useless now though; they'd obviously be going home.

David Blakeman had already suggested this, but the sight of Colin in tears and the wailing, terrified Alison brought an abrupt end to Grierson's ravings. He turned sharply away from them and was staring through a window, running his hands distractedly through his silky hair, and muttering to himself.

"I think it really would be best if we abandoned the whole project and I took the family home," Mr Blakeman repeated in a tight, controlled voice.

To everyone's astonishment, Grierson wouldn't hear of it. He suddenly turned round and came up to the painter, seized his hand and began to pump it, as if greeting a long-lost friend, stretching out his left arm to try and include Colin and Oliver in the circle of forgiveness. But the two boys had already backed away suspiciously and were standing by the open door. How could anyone change his tune so completely, in a matter of minutes?

Grierson was now actually apologizing for his fiendish temper, explaining how this break-in had been the last straw. He'd had some very bad news that week which had "knocked him sideways". Mr Blakeman, still very icy, asked him what was wrong. Bad news of his daughter perhaps? Or a death in the family?

Oh no, the man explained dismissively, nothing like that. It was bad *financial* news, some investment had gone disastrously wrong, and he stood to lose a lot of money. The three children looked at one another in disgust. *Money!* Why didn't Dad just tell him it was all over, then they could go down to the dungeons and start packing?

But Mr Grierson was subtle. He was a smoother talker than David Blakeman, and a faster thinker. He'd already assumed the row was finished and that they'd all stay on. Today he'd no business meetings, so, while the rooms were being set to rights, why didn't they all come with him, on a tour of his lands and properties? He could take them through some lovely countryside. There was room for everyone in the Range Rover, and they could find a beach for swimming, and he knew of a very good place for lunch. It would all be on him, naturally.

"I don't want to come," Colin said coldly, from the doorway. "Long car journeys make me feel sick. I'd rather stay round here."

"So would I," said Prill, detaching herself from Alison and going over to him. "Come on, let's get a picnic and go out for the day *on our own*." The next minute she was clattering after her brother down the cold back stairs.

Oliver hung back. He saw Hugo Grierson flush a dark angry pink and inspect his long finger nails for non-existent dirt. To his surprise he heard Mr Blakeman agree, coolly, to delay their departure for a few days, and see what he could do with the portrait. Yes, he'd certainly accept his invitation for this morning. The weather was beautiful and he'd welcome the chance to relax and enjoy the country. He ignored Grierson's hints about increasing his fee for the painting "if only he would reconsider".

Outside the door, Oliver heard Grierson say "Forgive and forget." The man talked like a romantic novel, it was embarrassing. What he couldn't understand was how quickly his uncle had given in, bending to Grierson's will like a straw in the wind, as if he was afraid of him.

"He's got the devil in him." That was what Duncan Ross had said. There was a great force in the man's personality, and Mr Blakeman had crumpled before it. But his uncle wasn't usually a weak and feeble "yes man"; he'd lost his temper more than once, with Oliver, and it hadn't been at all pleasant.

What was happening to Grierson? The boy believed that some deadly force had got him in its grip, and that he wasn't really in control of his own behaviour any more. There were traces of what he was, in his face, when you looked at him secretly. Oliver did that to people quite often and he pitied this man because, underneath everything, he saw he was terribly afraid. Behind all the noise and shouting there was guilt and terror in his soul, and a helplessness that verged almost on despair.

Chapter Fourteen

Breakfast was a very silent meal. The three children agreed on the stairs not to tell Aunt Phyllis exactly what had happened. "If we do, she'd go straight up and make a scene," Oliver said anxiously. "She'll give her notice and I'll have to go home then, even if you two don't."

"But wouldn't you rather go, Oll, after the way he treated you?" Colin asked, in a queer strained voice. He was very embarrassed about bursting into tears because of Grierson; what he'd actually wanted to do was to beat the man up.

"No, not *now*," the small boy said emphatically.

"What do you mean, what's different *now*?"

"I– we— " Oliver shot a look at Prill. "There's a lot to tell you, but I don't think we should talk in this house."

"Why? Do you think it's bugged?" Colin managed a weak grin.

"He obviously eavesdrops. He knew we called the place Castle Dracula, didn't he? I think we should get right away, before we have any discussions."

"But your mother's bound to ask what happened up there," Prill pointed out. "What are you going to say?"

"Nothing. Let's leave it to your father."

"But he'll tell her. He was hopping mad, you know."

"He *won't*. He's *scared* of Grierson, he'll fall in with him, you'll see. He's a very persuasive character," Oliver muttered mysteriously. Aggie Ross was stronger than both of them.

Oliver was absolutely right. David Blakeman didn't tell Aunt Phyllis about Grierson's attack on her son, that he had been flung across the room, and narrowly escaped having all his bones broken. He made light of the man's outburst and concentrated on the mess in the library, and on who could have done such a thing. It was uncanny, almost as if he was under some kind of spell.

The two adults sat over the teapot and speculated about who could have smashed the windows. Oliver listened in disgust. Grown-ups could be so *stupid*. There was no way such huge stones could have been flung at the glass from ground level. That was why Grierson had been so enraged by Colin, who was simply telling him what he already knew.

As soon as they dared, they slipped away to talk about the whole thing in private. Oliver, snooping round Lagg, had discovered an old hayloft over the saw mill. It was warm up there, among the big, scratchy bales, and quiet because no one had turned up yet to start the machinery. They got up by a wooden ladder. Jessie stood at the bottom and whined in frustration, then she took one huge flying leap and landed on Prill, scattering straw in all directions and yelping triumphantly.

"Shut up, dog," ordered Colin, "or it's *kennel time*."

Jessie stopped barking. She hated that nasty stone hut she had to sleep in. She burrowed into the bales, getting comfortable, hoping they might all go away soon, and forget her. It was much better here.

Prill let Oliver do most of the talking, but as he droned on and on, it was obvious that Colin was getting more and more bewildered. She could see that none of it made sense yet, at least, that none of it quite fitted together.

"That's why we mustn't go home now," Oliver was saying, "however foul Grierson is. We *must* find out what's going on."

"Well, it's a *poltergeist*," Colin answered, in a flat sort of voice, though secretly he felt rather excited. "It's a spirit of some kind, isn't it? One that flings things around. That's what you're saying."

"Ye–es," Oliver replied reluctantly. "Except... well, it's more complicated than that. First, why has it started up again, I mean, why *now*? And second, where did it come from in the first place? I think," he went on owlishly, answering his own questions, "that it's something we've done."

"Us?" said Colin. "You mean, you still think it's something to do with moving those stones?" He pulled a face. Oliver was always rather too anxious to make his theories fit. He wasn't agreeing to all this, not yet.

"I keep thinking," said Oliver, "about the time they were digging the Underground, near our house. A lot of the men on that job just gave up, you know. They'd gone very deep, and it frightened them down there."

"What did?"

"Just a horrible, evil *atmosphere*. And eventually they found a lot of skeletons. Dozens of them. They'd uncovered a plague pit, where they'd buried a lot of the victims."

"Ugh," said Prill.

"But nothing was flung around?" Colin wanted to know.

"No, that's why Lagg is quite different. Obviously we've disturbed something evil here too, but I think it's a particular person. Look at those marks on your dad's painting."

"You mean someone with a grudge against Grierson?"

"Yes, well, against the family."

"But there are *two* people, Oliver," Prill reminded him. "We've agreed on that."

She explained what she thought about the gentle singer to Colin, but the very look on his face told her that he was not convinced either. "So we've got a double haunting. Is that what you're saying?"

"I suppose I am," she said in a small voice, "something good, and something very bad, at war with one another."

There was silence, then Colin said, "No, no, Prill. It's just too fantastic."

"But you heard that singing, and you heard that awful laughing in the woods. You were the *first* to hear that. And you saw how all the bushes had been burned.

"Yes, but all that can be *explained*. I don't know what Oliver's found out about witches, but they're only people's theories after all. The woods go on for miles, there might be all sorts of cranks in them, like that loony who left us on the island."

Neither Prill nor Oliver said anything. That "loony" was the person who'd turned the bread all bloody, and the person who'd terrified Aunt Phyllis and wrecked Grierson's room. It could obviously assume any shape it fancied, or stay invisible.

"We should find out more about that stake," Colin said decisively. "It's the stake that really bugs Mr Grierson. We must find out what happened there."

"It was a death," Oliver reminded him. "The Rosses told us that. There's quicksand on that beach. Perhaps someone was sucked underneath and drowned."

"But why should the Rosses keep it up like they do if it's just the scene of an accident? I think it must have been a *murder*," Prill whispered emphatically.

"This is getting us nowhere," Oliver said, suddenly closing his little notebook and pushing it into his trouser pocket. "We're obviously not going to get anything more out of the Rosses. Come on, I'm going to see Granny MacCann. Mother's made a cake or something and she wants it taking down there. At least *she'll* talk to us."

CHAPTER FIFTEEN

They all went in the end but, in spite of Aunt Phyllis's present of freshly-baked cakes and scones, their visit was not a success. When they knocked on the door they obviously woke the old woman from a deep sleep. She seemed confused by Oliver's immediate stream of questions about Grierson and the history of Lagg. Her old cat had gone missing and it was this that was uppermost in her mind.

"Dandy," she kept uttering sadly. "Ma puir wee Dandy. Hasna' bin seen these three days, the puir wee beastie."

The two Blakemans were rather disgusted with Oliver. He talked enough about understanding elderly people when it suited him, and enjoyed reminding them of how he lived with old folk all the time, and knew their little ways, yet he wouldn't accept that Granny MacCann seemed to be having an off day. He'd come to get information, and that was all he seemed to care about. When it became evident that the old lady was having what his mother called a muzzy spell, and was going to be no use, he got up and announced abruptly that he was going home.

This seemed to wake Granny MacCann up slightly.

She got to her feet, put a kettle on to boil, and offered him one of his own cakes. "Bide a wee while, laddie," she said, the old cracked face breaking quite suddenly into a disarming smile. But Oliver was already halfway through the door. He had a serious set look on his pinched little face, and his pale blue eyes were very intent, behind the round black spectacles.

Prill knew perfectly well he wasn't going back to Lagg, though he was certainly anxious to get away somewhere, and he obviously wanted to go alone. He really was infuriating. One minute you felt quite close to him, the next he'd gone all mysterious and sneaky. Something new was on his mind. She could tell that by the way he hurried off, hardly bothering to say goodbye.

Prill was very uneasy in the tiny cottage. In spite of the old lady's warming smile she still looked horribly like a witch of fairy tale. She didn't quite trust Granny MacCann, or the shrivelled fingers that played with the string of shrunken red berries that hung round her scraggy neck. It was very hard not to suspect that she dabbled in what Oliver's witch book called The Black Art.

For once, Colin was subtler than his cousin. He didn't actually ask the old woman any questions, he simply described the recent goings on at Lagg Castle. The more she heard, the more old Granny perked up. "Aye, aye," she kept repeating. " 'Tis just what A tel't ye, the De'il's after auld Hughie the noo; tis young Aggie Ross. I'm tellin' ye." She laughed wickedly. "Och, aye," she went on. "I wairned ye. Ye shouldna hae meddled with the stanes. Aye, she's a wicket, wicket lassie that yin. Och, ma puir wee Dandy..."

The old woman rocked herself, and closed her eyes. Colin made up the fire, and poked it, and Granny MacCann moaned gently in the blaze. She still wore the jazzy striped legwarmers, but the cottage felt cold. In repose, the bristly pointed chin and the great hooked nose looked more terrifying than ever.

"Let's go," Prill whispered. "I hate it here."

Now he'd heard about Aggie Ross from someone other than Oliver Colin was quite content to shut the door quietly and follow his sister down the path. He was feeling rather pleased with himself. They'd scored over that clever cousin of theirs. *They* could report to *him* now. The old woman had confirmed all Oliver's theories, and he'd not been there to listen.

"Remember that house in South London," he said, as they walked quickly along the forest path. "Remember the furniture that kept being moved around, and the windows that got broken?"

"Yes, and it was burned down in the end," Prill reminded him. "What if *she* burns Lagg down?"

"Wicket" Aggie Ross. Granny MacCann had spoken as if it was the girl next door, not some restless, mischievous spirit, centuries old, that had been released from the past. Somehow, her chatty way of talking had made it all much worse.

"*Ross*," Colin said loudly. "Those two up at Ramshaws must know *something*. Why keep up a memorial to somebody as wicked as that? They can't exactly be proud of her."

And she was wicked, Colin didn't doubt that now. He only had to think of his first day in the woods. He remembered the blood-curdling laughter echoing through the trees, and the staggering weight that had leapt so suddenly on to his back, knocking all the breath out of him. Oliver *was* on to something, in believing it was all tied up with that old well at Lochashiel. When they got home they must tell him exactly what Granny MacCann had said. No doubt he'd be delighted to have his theories supported by the old woman. That awful smug look would creep across his pasty face, his special "told you so" expression, reserved for his cloddish cousins. Well, they'd just have to put up with it. Deciding what to do next was the most important thing. They were all in this together.

Oliver had been poking about at Lochashiel. There'd been no rain at all but the ground they'd uncovered was quite wet, and very obviously a circle. A spring must be bubbling away somewhere under the rubble that people had thrown down the well, over the years.

Oliver was always prepared for any emergency, even though his mother had never allowed him to be in the Scouts. She didn't think he was strong enough for all their antics. He'd been going through the mud wearing a pair of old rubber gloves, feeling for more bits and pieces with his thin fingers. He was patient and methodical, and at the end of an hour's work a polythene bag lay on the grass full of small yellowish bones.

He would take them home, wash them, and put them with the others. Then he would try to reassemble them all into some recognizable shape. What he really needed was a book on natural history, or *perhaps* – Oliver shivered slightly at the thought – a volume about the human body. It would be much quicker to sneak up to Mr Grierson's rooms and see what was on his shelves than to try and get to a public library from here...

It was late when he left Lochashiel. Mother would tick him off if he missed dinner, so he set off at a run. The grass woodlands didn't scare Oliver at all, and he soon found a short cut down to the road, a steep rocky track under the Crag, overgrown with brambles. If he could push his way through it would save him a good ten minutes.

As he dropped down through the trees something bounded across his path and sat on its haunches very near him. It was the big hare they'd seen near Hag's Folly. Oliver identified it by the curious white mark splashed on its back. It was looking straight at him.

"Shoo!" he called out, a strange coldness creeping over him. "Shoo! get away!" He picked up a stone and threw it. The hare didn't budge. Oliver threw another stone, then he made a run at it. "Get away from me," he yelled, starting to panic. He had the same fear of this creature that he had of small, yappy dogs, a secret terror that they would suddenly go for him and sink their nasty little teeth into a bare leg or arm.

The hare turned slowly, almost insolently, and lolloped off into the trees. But even now Oliver felt that its huge dark eyes were on him, that it hadn't gone very far but that it was hiding somewhere nearby, mocking him as the thorns tore at his legs, and he scratched his hands on matted brambles.

But what he saw next drove the strange creature, and his fear of it, clean out of his head. On a bush, in a small clearing where two tracks crossed, he found the remains of a small animal. It looked as if it had been neatly jointed by a very sharp knife but as if, afterwards, some madman had taken over and played lunatic games with it. A fly-blown bloody mess in the middle of the crossing was all that remained of the animal's insides and lumps of black and white fur had been flung all over the clearing. There was a tail on the ground and, stuck on a rotten fencing post, staring at him mournfully, was the creature's head. It was Granny MacCann's old cat. It was Dandy.

For a few seconds Oliver stood there, frozen. Only his eyes moved, flickering from the head, to the blood and pulp on the ground, to the ragged stump of tail. Then he turned away and was suddenly very sick into the bracken.

None of it could be left here. On their next visit to Granny's Prill and Colin might easily stumble upon this track, if they looked for a short cut. Besides, his instinct was to bury everything at once. Poor Granny MacCann must never know what had happened to her moth-eaten, mangy old cat.

He acted quickly, pulling the muddy rubber gloves back on and scooping a shallow hole in some soft earth, under one of the bushes. He threw everything in, fur, guts, what remained of the poor cat's heart and liver. Half-closing his eyes and scarcely drawing breath he detached the stringy tail and flung that in too. Seconds later the awful staring head had followed, and Oliver was stamping violently on the little patch of soil, his stomach still churning and a horrible tightness in his throat.

He wanted to get away from that bloody crossroads now. Overdone meat and two veg from that fault-finding mother of his waiting impatiently at Lagg suddenly seemed wildly attractive. But before he left Oliver did something most uncharacteristic. He hated Sundays and he hated the hours he had to spend with his mother in St Matthew's, surely the coldest, dreariest church in London. Nevertheless, he found a bit of string in his pocket, tied two twigs together to make a tiny cross, and stuck it firmly into Dandy's grave. The act tugged him back to earliest childhood, to the death of his hamster. He'd done that then, in their tiny London garden. Ma had never allowed him another pet, he'd cried so much.

As he hurried through the trees he sang in a loud tuneless voice, a voice that sounded half-hysterical. "Glad that I live am I," he bawled, "That the sky is blue; Glad for the country lanes And the fall of dew…" He chose the only hymn he liked because it was so thoroughly cheerful.

But whoever was listening didn't like it at all, nor did they like the boy's harsh, unmusical singing, and they certainly hadn't liked the cross. All the way to Lagg there was an undertow of low animal growling in the trees. Fortunately for Oliver he was singing far too loud to hear it.

CHAPTER SIXTEEN

He brooded on what had happened all through the meal, but he decided not to tell the others, not yet anyway. He did want to talk to them though, about going up to Ramshaws, to see if they could find out a bit more about young Aggie Ross, and about the stake.

After what Granny MacCann had revealed, the Blakemans had planned to steal away with Oliver, straight after dinner, and have a conference in the hayloft, but Aunt Phyllis thwarted their plans. She was going upstairs to help clear up the library, now the glass had been replaced. But she didn't want Alison. The wretched child had refused to go on the car ride – that was Colin's fault, she informed him, saying car journeys made him sick. She'd trotted round after her aunt all morning, cherry-cheeked and healthy, saying "'Ick, 'ick," and putting her tongue out for inspection. Aunt Phyllis had had quite enough of Alison.

They were dispatched for a good long walk with the dog and the toddler and told to stay out till five o'clock. Tea was at half-past. Afterwards they could all play Scrabble together, or they might prefer to go to their rooms and read. Aunt Phyllis believed in resting after any kind of physical exertion. It was going to be a really jolly evening.

The tide was high, so instead of the beach they took Alison to Hag's Folly. She ran all over the place as they walked through the woods, and there was no chance to talk properly. The Rosses' blue dinghy was pulled up on the shingle and they went over in that. This time there were no alarms, except when Jessie decided to leap from the boat and swim ashore. Alison tried to go after her.

"Poor, poor Jessie," she wailed as the dog ducked under the water. But she was waiting for them on the island, and showered them all liberally as she shook herself dry. Then she was off, nose down, tail flapping wildly. She remembered Hag's Folly, its nice welcoming smells, and that goat.

To Prill it was a different place today, there was no mystery about it. She would not see the young woman, with her pet on a string, and there would be no sign of the withered ferryman. As they wandered about, Colin and Oliver down in the dank cellar and she, hand in hand with Alison, scrambling about on the walls and chucking pebbles into the water, it was hard to believe the terrors of their last visit.

"She's not here," she said dreamily, chewing on a piece of Aunt Phyllis's flapjack. They'd come together for a snack on the little shingle beach, and they were all skimming pebbles across the water.

"Who's not here? What are you talking about?

Don't, Allie!" Colin brushed wet sand from his jeans and looked at his sister, frowning. "You mean the... the, er, woman who sings?" He opened his mouth, then shut it again. You had to be careful with Prill, once she became really convinced about something. "It could have been a radio," he said rather feebly.

"At three in the morning? It *wasn't*. It was that woman, the woman I saw *here*, at the top of the cellar steps." Prill buried her face in Jessie's silky coat, feeling confused and stupid. Colin thought she was imagining things, as usual.

"Aggie Ross?"

"No, no, *no*!" Prill yelled at him in frustration, and the dog jumped away in alarm. "Aggie Ross is *wicked*, Granny MacCann told us that, you heard her yourself. This girl's not, she's... she's a *holy* sort of person. Oh, I just can't *explain*."

"*Girl?*" Colin repeated. "You said *woman* a minute ago."

"Well, she's not very old, about eighteen I should think, and she's got this little goat. She takes it about with her on a string."

Prill felt hot and embarrassed and she wasn't saying any more. She got up and wandered down to the water's edge. A hazy sunshine filtered down and it was all unutterably still. The small mountains might have been painted on the greying sky and the loch was like glass, apart from the odd plopping of a fish.

"The old woman confirmed everything you told us," Colin said to Oliver, in a low voice. "Just thought you'd want to know. She said those stones should never have been touched, and that the devil was after Grierson now. 'Auld Hughie' she called him." He smiled.

Oliver didn't. He was still worrying about Prill, and the apparition on the island. How stupid of Colin to suggest that someone so harmless could be a fiend like Aggie Ross. His trouble was that he never thought things *through*.

Prill felt Lagg's woodlands were different, as they walked back. This afternoon there seemed no need to hurry through them; it was hard to speed Alison along anyway, she would insist on stopping to pick things up and tried, hopelessly to get up some of the trees.

The trip had felt so peaceful, so *normal*, that Prill breathed more deeply at last and felt that whatever dark thing had been dogging them had gone to earth at last. Oliver, had he known what she was thinking, would have warned her of just the opposite. Rain was on its way, possibly storms, hence this unnatural calm. The picture imprinted on his mind was of Granny MacCann's dead cat. He was keeping that strictly to himself. It was his belief that Aggie Ross, having completed that monstrous act, had withdrawn, to gather her resources together. She'd be back before long, and worse than ever.

Aunt Phyllis greeted them with the news that Grierson's wonderful new Range Rover had broken down sixty miles from home.

"He has friends, as it happens. Friends with a small estate quite near where they're stranded. So they're stopping there for the night. They'll be back some time in the morning."

Friends, Colin was thinking sourly, *friends*! I don't believe he's got any friends. They'll be stinking rich too. He'll just do business deals with them.

He was annoyed because his father had talked of borrowing one of the cars and taking them all to the late showing of the new Indiana Jones film in Dumfries. Now that plan had been knocked squarely on the head. The alternative, Scrabble with his aunt, didn't appeal at all. His headache had come back. They were getting steadily more frequent, and much more painful. All Aunt Phyllis could suggest was aspirin and an early night. She wasn't very concerned about the girl's aches and pains either.

Prill's sense of well-being had been short-lived, she'd begun to feel distinctly odd at the tea table and, as the evening wore on, she grew steadily worse. She kept getting a strange tightness in her chest, as if it was bound fast with cords, and at the same time, out of a clear blue sky, great waves of cold kept sweeping over her, from nowhere. At these times she heard her sweet voice most clearly, but there was a greater sadness in it now, and a growing desperation.

Aunt Phyllis put all these strange sensations down to bad dreams. If it was Mrs Blakeman's flu bug they'd agreed they would dose her, and wait for it to develop. Colin's headaches were part of the same thing, no doubt.

"I'm not worrying your father unnecessarily," Aunt Phyllis announced crisply, doling the pills out. She would have been rather more sympathetic except that it was Sunday tomorrow, and she was plotting and scheming to get them all to church. She was a woman who pursued one idea at a time and, although it was annoying to be left single-handed with four children, it would give her a golden opportunity to get a bit of religion into them. Mr and Mrs Blakeman were far too free and easy on this matter, in Aunt Phyllis's view. Those children were going to end up little heathens.

The church was at Lochbean, a scattering of granite cottages strung along a lonely road about a mile from Lagg. Alison didn't go with them. Aunt Phyllis disapproved of toddlers disrupting church services. Instead she was to be deposited at Granny MacCann's.

The Blakeman children were aghast at this arrangement. Granny MacCann, that smelly, doddery old woman? Prill tried to object but Aunt Phyllis soon silenced her. True, the old lady wasn't too well physically but she was certainly in her right mind. She'd got seven children and fifteen grandchildren, many of whom were left at her cottage for the odd hour in perfect safety. Mr

Blakeman knew about the arrangement apparently, and was quite happy with it. Besides, Prill herself had commented on how Alison adored Granny MacCann.

"So there's no more to be said, is there?" snapped Aunt Phyllis, pulling on black gloves and adjusting an amazing hat.

"No," Prill said meekly. There never was, with Aunt Phyllis, and she felt too unwell to argue. The awful tight feeling hadn't gone away. In the night it had been almost as if she was being choked, or suffocated.

It was a Communion service, and all the way along the road there were mutterings of "We won't know what to do", from the Blakemans.

"Just sit in the pew and follow the book," Oliver whispered glumly. He'd just been confirmed so he'd have to go up with his mother, to receive the bread and wine, but he hoped desperately that the service wouldn't drag on and on, like it did at home. It had rained in the night, and the earth was fresh and beautiful. Nobody really wanted to spend long hours in a church on a day like this.

The congregation was made up of seven people, the party from Lagg and three old ladies who sat in a line in the very back pew. Aunt Phyllis propelled the children up to the front, smiled faintly at the clergyman, and sat down. He was a small, saintly-looking man with a cloud of silver hair, John Ballantyne, known locally as "auld Jockie".

In a dusty corner someone was playing a harmonium very badly. The minister moved about slowly, preparing the communion. Aunt Phyllis sank to her knees and the three children stared round.

It was a tiny church, granite like the rest of the village, and the heavy oak door had been wedged open, letting the sunlight spill upon the rows of polished pews. Prill rather wished they'd shut that door. A coldness had swept in with them, the same dankness she always felt in Lagg's woodland. Even before the old man had said a word the girl felt distinctly uneasy.

Aunt Phyllis got up from her knees, settled herself in the pew, and sniffed. This place was damp, and no wonder. Water had obviously got in. In one corner was a great black stain. If this was *her* church she'd do a bit of fund-raising. It couldn't be safe, just leaving it like that. Dampness led to dry-rot and she certainly knew all about that. Think of the mess at 9 Thames Terrace, and dear Stanley, coping on his gas-ring.

Prill was also looking at the stain. Was it her imagination, or had it moved slightly? She looked all round. It must be the sunlight filtering through the plain glass windows, or the trees waving outside. Perhaps she just needed her eyes testing. A stain couldn't suddenly shift its position across the floor. But Oliver had seen it too, and he knew exactly what had happened, and who had followed them in. Thank goodness they were near the minister and his table, that place of safety.

The minute the "Our Father" began, a strange noise started up somewhere quite near them. Old Jock Ballantyne carried on steadily in his soft Scots voice, but Oliver was listening intently. It was a light, lowish voice, a woman's not a man's. Sometimes it seemed to be talking an unintelligible gibberish, at others it growled, like a dog.

Aunt Phyllis appeared to have heard nothing amiss. She was poring over her book, and following the service with one gloved forefinger. Prill took in nothing, her eyes were riveted on the great dark stain. As she looked it seemed to get bigger, to take on substance like coarse black cloth. Could it be the old man's cope, flung carelessly aside as he arrived, hurrying to get the church ready? As she stared she saw something detach itself from the blackness and hop across the flagged floor, and under a kneeler. It was an enormous toad.

"*Ugh*," said Colin in disgust. "This place needs Rentokil, or something. I've heard of churches infested by mice, but *toads*… honestly."

He nudged the kneeler aside with his foot. It was all Prill could do to suppress a scream, but there was no sign of the great slimy creature in the dark of the pew. "It obviously doesn't like the music," whispered Colin with a giggle, as the decrepit organist wheezed into action with the harmonium. "I don't blame it. What a racket."

The Psalm for the day had a very old tune. Prill liked

singing and she enjoyed the strong, plain music, in spite of the dreadful organ. The familiar words were twisted round curiously though, to fit the beat:

> *"I to the hills will lift mine eyes:*
> *From whence doth come mine aid.*
> *My safety cometh from the Lord*
> *Who heaven and earth hath made...*
> *The Lord shall keep thy soul; He shall*
> *Preserve thee from all ill;*
> *Henceforth thy going out and in*
> *God keep for ever will..."*

A sweet voice was singing the Psalm with them, not loud, but making every word ring out in the cold, damp little church. Prill turned right round to survey the congregation but was immediately yanked into position again by an embarrassed Aunt Phyllis. She hadn't seen anyone, apart from the three old ladies mumbling over their books, but the singing couldn't possibly have come from them, they were too old. None of them could have produced that steady young voice.

She was here, the woman from Hag's Folly, Prill was sure of it. She felt calmer and the awful tightness had gone away, quite suddenly. She took deep, slow breaths, smelling the familiar country smell as it mingled with the mustiness of the church, hearing the voice as it mingled with her own, feeling safe for the first time.

As they sang, the old man moved about at the front, preparing the bread and wine. He was extremely shaky and feeble, eighty if he was a day, and at one point they saw the communion bread flutter to the ground in small flakes. In embarrassment he bent down, and gathered it all together again. The hymn was over and the congregation waited patiently for the service to go on.

It was then the church darkened suddenly. The sun must have clouded over, and a cold gust blew sharply down the central aisle, riffling the pages of the prayer books and raising the strip of red carpet in little waves. Outside, Jessie, tied firmly to a fence and patiently waiting, began a loud barking.

Aunt Phyllis let the three old ladies go to the tiny communion rail first, then, with the two Blakemans looking on, she shoved Oliver out of the pew and prodded him towards the front.

"He doesn't want to *go*," Colin whispered. "Look at him, he's as white as a sheet. What's the matter with him?"

Oliver was in a cold sweat. When the old man placed the chalice in his hands the communion bread was still on his tongue; it lay there like a piece of cold rubber and he was quite unable to dissolve it and swallow it down. He took the silver cup but simply held it, watching the dark wine swill round against the gilded inside. It was a beautiful plain chalice, centuries old probably, and no doubt worth thousands of pounds.

The old man was pronouncing the familiar sentences over him but Oliver, trying to raise the now leaden cup to his lips, heard nothing. He only tasted a drop, then he began to sway about; the cup fell through his fingers, crashing on to the stone steps, and rolling about the floor, and the wine spilled out of it and over the damp flags in a thin red stream. There had been no wine in that chalice, only blood.

It seemed, as Oliver fell backwards and passed into unconsciousness, that the whole church was blood, great thick gouts of it on the floor and the furnishings, and on the people, and that the altar, where the old man now stood with the dented chalice in his hand, was mobbed with terrible black shadows.

He was only out for a few seconds. Colin had leapt forward and caught him as he sank down, just saving him from gashing his head on a corner of the steps. Aunt Phyllis was in control in seconds, pink with embarrassment, her felt hat flapping, thrusting his head down between his knees and keeping up a running commentary about "overtired" and "reading into the night", and "coming out without a proper breakfast inside you". All Oliver could hear, as his swimming head broke the surface of consciousness again, was a peal of high-pitched laughter that echoed round the church.

His mother took him firmly by the arm, mumbled her apologies to the old man, and marched him outside. "Damp," she was saying, "horribly damp. Gets on your chest and lungs. Fresh air needed, I'd say."

Jessie was overjoyed to see them, and yelped to be released from the fence. But she'd had quite a profitable time during the church service. Someone had scattered bread all round her, for birds presumably, but quite underestimating this greedy creature's capacity for gobbling up anything that resembled food.

It was Oliver who saw what she was doing.

"Don't!" he cried out in horror. "Don't, *don't*, Jessie..." It was too late. The big setter was licking her lips at the last mouthful of holy bread that had been scooped from the church floor and flung at her feet like so much scrap paper. There wasn't a crumb left.

Prill and Colin exchanged puzzled looks. Oliver clearly wasn't himself, he must be feeling a bit light-headed. Jessie ate all kinds of funny things, she had an iron constitution. A few bits of bread wouldn't do her any harm.

But their young cousin knew otherwise. He knew exactly what it meant, and what Aggie Ross had done. The dog would become Her Creature, Jessie was in her power, and the witch could do exactly what she wanted with her. What on earth was going to happen?

CHAPTER SEVENTEEN

"They were *both* there," Prill whispered in Oliver's ear. He still looked very white and feeble, and she'd got her arm firmly through his. They were all walking through the woods, back to Granny MacCann's, but Colin and Aunt Phyllis had rushed on ahead. Because of Oliver's faint, Alison had now been there longer than an hour, and Aunt Phyllis was worried.

"I only felt *her*," Oliver said shakily. "It's not that I don't believe you, but I only felt *her*. She... she picks on people, have you noticed? It was me today, and if we hadn't got outside... ugh, I daren't think what might have happened."

He just couldn't tell Prill about witches and their Black Masses; how, in times past, they'd broken into churches and turned the crosses upside down, and said all the prayers back to front; how they stole babies and killed them, and used their blood for wine in their terrible rites, how they danced on the altar and mocked at all that was most precious and holy.

There had been the beginnings of all that, in Lochbean church, and if he hadn't fainted away, and if old Jock Ballantyne hadn't been a strong man, a man of prayer... Oliver shuddered to think what might have happened next.

"*She* picks on people too," Prill said thoughtfully, though it was the wrong way to describe what that gentle, holy presence was doing. It was because *she'd* been with them in the church that Aggie Ross hadn't prevailed.

It was pandemonium at Granny MacCann's. The old lady was sitting outside in the sun, in a wicker chair, with Alison at her feet, happily grubbing about in the dirt, but inside the house the fat, slovenly young woman they'd seen on their first visit was having loud hysterics. "Where's ma wee Jennie?" the voice kept bawling. "Where's ma puir wee Jennie?"

Aunt Phyllis was doing her very best with Granny MacCann, who was clearly bewildered by the noise her granddaughter was making. She thought the problem was about Alison. "Why, she's here by me, the bonnie wee thing," she kept saying plaintively.

"No, Granny, the *baby*. The baby your granddaughter left here for a few minutes," Aunt Phyllis shouted in her ear. She assumed all old people were deaf, though Mrs MacCann's hearing was very acute.

"I can hear ye!" Granny shouted back snappily. "Dinna screech, wumman!"

The fat girl suddenly burst out of the cottage door and yelled at the bewildered grandmother. "Whar's Jennie, for God's sake? No' three months auld and ye cann tend her! Ye said ye'd look after the wee'n while I ran hame…"

A torrent of abuse followed, in broad Scots, and Aunt Phyllis stood helplessly in the middle of it. In a terror of anticipation, Oliver crept inside the cottage, a horrible line from *Macbeth* pounding through his head. "Finger of a birth-strangled babe," a voice kept whispering. She must have been *here* too. Witches needed little babies, they used that fine skin to make bridles, with which they harnessed the wind. Aggie Ross, having made havoc at Lochbean, had crept along here and spirited poor little Jennie away, while the old woman dozed…

Inside, nothing looked very different. None of the clutter had been meddled with, or flung about. Oliver slipped outside again and peered round carefully. There were no scorch marks in the tangled little garden, and the grove of young mountain ash rose up graceful and whole, their pale, delicate branches patterning the small burn that flowed by the gate. *Of course*, a witch couldn't cross running water, and those rowan trees must have been planted to keep evil *away*. And Granny MacCann was wearing the shrivelled rowan berries on a string round her neck. How stupid of anyone to suggest she might be a witch herself.

A man had come into the garden and was trying to calm down the overwrought granddaughter. Granny, when she wasn't moaning about her "puir wee Dandy," was saying, "the wee'n's wi' Elspeth Macdonald, I'm tellin' ye." Aunt Phyllis pieced together that Mrs Macdonald had taken the baby back down to the village, and left a note to say so. The harassed little man who'd just walked up the path was obviously the husband, and was explaining what had happened to his sobbing wife. The note had been left while Granny dozed, with Alison asleep on her lap. No doubt the wretched child had later destroyed it, as she destroyed most things. There were suspicious scraps of paper under the wicker chair.

What a mix-up. It hadn't occurred to Aunt Phyllis that the old woman might nod off on duty. It should have done, of course. She wouldn't let Granny MacCann babysit again. She gathered the children together and hastily pushed them through the gate. Oliver went slowly, feeling weak at the knees. It wasn't the faintness any more, he felt light-headed with sheer relief that "ma puir wee Jennie" was safe.

Aunt Phyllis had this infuriating knack of deciding what was best for everybody. When they reached Lagg, Mr Grierson's Range Rover was drawn up outside the house.

"They're back," she announced, putting Alison's sticky paw firmly into Prill's hand, "Go and find your father, the three of you. No doubt he'd like to see you at once. Oliver and I have got things we can do in the kitchen. *Come along, Oliver.*"

It was thoughtful of her, but she always sounded so bossy, and after all that had happened both Prill and Colin were desperate to talk to Oliver. He pulled a helpless face at the retreating Blakemans and followed his mother down into the dungeons. She'd mixed some bread dough before setting off for church, and she stood at the old scrubbed table, kneading it violently, thinking about that missing baby and how she should never have arranged for old Granny to mind Alison. The floor of the outer scullery was a mass of muddy footprints. Oliver was instantly organized into mopping it over for her. He looked quite himself again now, and she quickly equipped him with bucket, mop and flowery apron. He set to work gloomily. Washing floors was the last thing he wanted to do just now, after the various shocks of the morning, but that was why Ma had made him do it. It was therapy. No time to brood on your ailments if you had muddy marks to slosh away at.

Meanwhile, in the main kitchen, she was listening to the radio. Some dialect programme, so broad Oliver could hardly understand it. Perhaps it was the local station, Radio Solway he thought it was called. It was a poetry programme, not his mother's cup of tea at all. *The Archers*, *Woman's Hour*, and the *Daily Service* were more her line. The voice was very high and thin, mocking almost. Oliver crept up to the scullery door and stood behind it, listening:

"We put this into this hame,
In our Lord the Devil's name;
The first hands that handle thee
Burned and scalded may they be…"

He peeped round the door and looked at the old portable radio. They'd brought it with them on the train. It wasn't even plugged in. His mother was humming to herself as she knocked the bread down and shaped the pieces of dough ready for the tins. She'd obviously heard nothing, and the sneaky little voice was fading away quickly now, into the trees, fading, till all that was left of it was a familiar thin squeal of laughter.

It wasn't until the dough had been set to rise again, and his mother was on her way back to Granny MacCann's to see that the old lady was all right after the upsets of the morning, that Oliver plucked up enough courage to lift the loose, rocking slab he'd discovered in the scullery. The surrounding stones were darkly spotted, he'd noticed, spots he couldn't remove with all his mopping, and under the slab itself he found what he knew must be there, a sloppy mealy mixture that appeared to be made of blood, bones, and hair. (He remembered that bloody loaf, with all the grit and hairs in it.)

The boy felt very sick. What he'd heard was a witch's spell. Some awful incantation must have been uttered over that loaf too, and if he didn't do something, this revolting mess would somehow end up in his mother's new bread, nicely rising on the stove. When she touched the loaves she'd get horribly burned. Aggie Ross would see to that. Oliver was quite certain about it.

"Please protect me," he said aloud, spreading out newspapers and spooning the sloppy red meal on to it. He rolled it up tight and thrust it on to the back of the kitchen fire. The dripping parcel burned sullenly and fitfully, with a horrible smell, and clouds of thick, greenish smoke billowed out into the room. Oliver poked at it, making sure it burned right through. Remembering all the horror stories he'd ever read he said firmly. "Be gone and give us peace, in Christ's name. Amen." As he did so he distinctly heard a low growling round his feet, like that of an angry dog.

When the thing was a heap of stinking embers Oliver was suddenly overcome with revulsion. The fire could go out now, for all he cared. He went outside, crossed the huge lawn, and slipped into the old walled garden that lay beyond the forbidden oak tree. It was full of flowers and bees, and sweet-smelling herbs. Oliver sat there for a long time, with his eyes closed, trying to blot out the picture of what he'd found under the flag-stone, trying to forget that fiendish growling noise, and that terrible smell from the fire.

He came back to the house just in time to see Mr Grierson disappearing down the drive in his Mercedes. The second floor rooms occupied by his uncle were empty, so were the dungeon bedrooms. Prill's camera had gone, and so had Colin's binoculars. It was rather mean of them all to vanish like that, without saying anything to him, but the empty house did give him one golden opportunity, so for once he didn't feel too peeved.

When he'd really set his mind on something, Oliver was quite fearless. The door to Grierson's suite was open, and he simply walked in. He began to look along the bookshelves. It was easy to find what he wanted. The library was carefully arranged according to subject, and there was even a small plan of it pinned to the inside of the door. There were five volumes of *Local History* and Oliver, not daring to stay too long, went straight to the indexes for the items he wanted; "Witchcraft" and "Grierson of Lagg".

But he was unlucky. In every case the relevant pages had been carefully removed. One went from 78 to 85, for example, another from 110 to 119. All traces of Grierson's evil ancestor had been wiped out, and anything Oliver might have gleaned about his witch-hunting exploits had vanished too. In only one case was there anything useful left. Just a couple of sentences, beginning in the middle. The heading at the top of the page was "Local Martyrs" and the words read "... *as a witch, 17th August 1685. At low tide the pathetic memorial may sometimes still be seen.*"

Oliver hunted round for a scrap of paper. He found a jotter on Grierson's desk and, as before, the red leather diary lay open next to it. The most recent entry was short. "*The poor creature comes and goes continually, with her prayers and singing. Must see Lawrence about a change of sleeping pill.*" Then in red, backwards, Oliver deciphered carefully, "*Will the Lord absent himself for ever, and will he be no more intreated? Is his mercy clean gone for ever, and is his promise come utterly to an end for ever more?*"

Oliver read the entry twice. Prill was right in her conviction that somebody else was haunting Lagg Castle, someone who meant them no harm. Mr Grierson wouldn't refer to an evil, blood-sucking she-devil as one who came and went "with her prayers and singing".

Pausing only to hide *A Short Handbook of Human Anatomy* under his sweater, he crept down the back stairs and went down to his bedroom. He slipped the book under the mattress, pushed a small notebook and pencil into the back pocket of his jeans, and in two minutes was on the woodland path, heading for Lagg's beach.

CHAPTER EIGHTEEN

As Oliver came out of the trees, he spotted his two cousins far out on the sand, near the black stake. His uncle was sitting in the dunes with Alison. She was playing roly poly, scrambling up to the top of a big sandy hillock then tumbling down, with giggles, into the great yellow crater below. The game stopped abruptly as Oliver wandered up. She'd just got a mouthful of sand and was now wailing dismally.

"Hello, Oliver," David Blakeman called out. "Sorry just to go off, but we couldn't find you anywhere. Did you find our note? I left it on the kitchen table."

"Oh, no, no I didn't," said Oliver. He'd avoided the kitchen after what he'd found under that flagstone. Until Aggie Ross was laid to rest he didn't think he'd feel safe anywhere in Lagg Castle, or in its woodlands either.

"You look stormy," his Uncle remarked, rocking the snivelling toddler and trying to extract the sand from her mouth. "You remind me of Mr Grierson. Cheer up."

"Heck, do I?" Oliver pulled himself together inside and squeezed a smile out. "I've been doing jobs for my mother and I – well, I did wonder where you'd all gone."

Mr Blakeman had been sitting staring out to sea, thinking about the last twenty-four hours. He hadn't enjoyed touring round with Hugo Grierson at all, and he suddenly spilled it all out to Oliver.

"He's so foul-tempered," he said, "so impatient with people. You should have heard him when his precious car broke down. He cursed everyone under the sun, and his language was quite unbelievable. Good job your Ma wasn't in earshot."

Oliver grinned. "Good thing she didn't see the way he treated me when the windows got broken. We'd have been back to London on the next train."

"I admired you for that, Oliver," Mr Blakeman said warmly, "keeping your cool. I didn't. You may have noticed."

Oliver went pink. He was rather fond of his Uncle David. "Well, somehow, in spite of everything, I feel sorry for Mr Grierson. It's almost as if, well, as if it's not his *fault*, if you know what I mean."

Mr Blakeman looked doubtful. "I do, in a way. He's had a sad time really. His wife dying so young like that, then the awful quarrel with his daughter." He paused, then he said thoughtfully, "But you know, I can't see any *need* for his pig-headed attitude there. He has *one* child, a daughter – all he's got in the world apparently – and he quarrels with her just because she wants to marry a farmer, and not just a quarrel either, a *feud*. What sort of man is he? Do you know, Oliver, that man's got a little grandson who he's never even *seen*. Can you believe that?"

"He'd love it at Lagg, wouldn't he?" Oliver said solemnly, thinking sadly of the great oak tree with its empty swings, and the dust-covered rocking horse up in Helen's room. "But isn't the husband related to Angus Ross? I'm sure Granny MacCann told Mother that. Isn't it because she married a *Ross*, all this hatred, I mean?"

His uncle looked at him. Oliver had put his finger on it as usual. He was an odd individual, in so many ways he was wise beyond his years; he listened, drew his own private conclusions, and never forgot anything.

"Nursing his wrath to keep it warm," quoted Mr Blakeman, cuddling Alison. "You're quite right, Oliver. He hates the whole Ross family, for some reason, and he treats that poor man Angus and his son abominably. The families have always clashed, apparently, I mean, right through the years, and I think that's why he won't let me borrow any books about the region. I imagine the Grierson side of the feud doesn't come out too well. He says the books are at the binders, or something. I don't believe a word of it. Do you?"

"No, I don't," muttered Oliver, standing up and looking along the beach. He was anxious to join the others, so he didn't elaborate, in case he got involved in a long conversation, but he had a strange, fluttery feeling inside. He was fascinated by what he'd just heard about Grierson and his missing books. Everything was beginning to slot slowly into place, like an enormous jigsaw puzzle.

Out by the stake, his two cousins appeared to have made a gigantic sand castle. They looked muddy, wet, and tired. Prill stood up when she saw him, her face strangely flushed, but Colin went on working, scooping up the sand and flinging it on to the pile behind him.

"Hardly any of it was exposed when we arrived," he explained. "I thought it was just a bit of rock at first. The sand's always shifting here, Duncan told me that. I suppose the only thing they could do would be to mount it permanently in concrete or something. But the tide would wash that away eventually."

He was kneeling at the edge of a wide, shallow hole. "I'd like Dad to see it," he said proudly, "but I wanted to uncover the whole thing first. Anyway, we've done it now. Look at that, Oll."

Oliver peered down into the hole. What they'd taken for a rock was in fact the corner of a flat stone slab. It was very long, and wide enough for several lines of writing. The deep-cut letters had been washed at by centuries of wind, sand, and water, and many were shapeless and hacked about. It was obvious, though, that people came here, whenever the tablet was exposed, to cut deeper into the letters so that the message on the stone would never be destroyed, just as they renewed the old wooden stake when it started to rot in the gales, and the keen salt wind.

Oliver knelt down, wiped the sand from his glasses, and read aloud, slowly:

"To the memory of Margrat Ross, age 18,
Daughter of Gilbert Ross of Lochbean,
Who was drouned August 17th, 1685.
Let earth and stone stil witnes beare
Their dyed a virgin martyre here,
Murdered for witchcraft's sin and shame,
Even though she worshipped God supreme.
Within the sea, tyed to a stake,
She suffered for Christ Jesus' sake.
The actors of this cruel crime
Were Grierson, Scott, Mackay, and Graham.
Neither young yeares nor tendre age
Could stop the fury of there rage."

There was a strong wind blowing in off the sea. Already the tablet was being splattered with wet sand, and Oliver looked out anxiously beyond the stake.

"The tide's coming in," he said, in a choked sort of voice, "I doubt if your dad'll get out to this in time. But *look*," he said, suddenly fishing in his back pocket and pulling out his notebook. "Look what I copied out, in Mr Grierson's library. The pathetic memorial! This is obviously it. *Look*, Grierson's is the first name mentioned, Grierson the Witch Finder; she was obviously one of his victims. No wonder Drac's so peculiar about the Rosses! It's wonderful, finding this. Congratulations!

But when he saw Prill's face he turned away

embarrassed. Her eyes had not moved from the letters on the slab, and her heart was full to bursting. Some of it made sense now. The woman on the island was Margaret Ross. That was why she had felt such holiness surrounding her, and why she'd heard the sweet, sad singing of those ancient hymns. That was why she'd had the sense that, wherever *Margaret* was, there was peace and goodness too.

And yet her name was *Ross*, and she'd been falsely accused of witchcraft. How could a girl like that have anything to do with the devilish Agnes, the fiend who was wreaking such havoc at Lagg?

"It's wonderful." Oliver's excitement jarred on her. Why had she died here? It wasn't wonderful at all, it was bloody and agonizing and terrible. Prill stood apart, weeping freely, and the spray from the incoming tide mingled with the tears as they ran down her face.

That night the three of them went up to Ramshaws again. They found Duncan on his own, listening to pop music and cleaning his father's guns. Angus was down at the pub in Kirkmichael.

He was very pleased to see them. He spent too many nights alone, and it made him broody.

"How did ye get awa?" he wanted to know. He obviously knew all about the strict Aunt Phyllis, and her Rules and Regulations.

"I said your dad had invited us up for... for a feast

of hare pie," Oliver said, flushing. He'd been so determined to see the Rosses, after what they'd uncovered on the beach, that he'd lied his head off to his mother, so many lies, he just didn't dare think about it. "I don't suppose you've caught it yet?"

"Och no," said Duncan. "It's queer. A've had twa shots at that canny wee beastie, and A've missed the both o'them. Now A've cleaned the guns A'll gang for her again. She's no' for ma *faither* to take!"

They were disappointed not to see Angus. When Oliver started his interrogation it was obvious that Duncan's knowledge was very patchy. He was more interested in the here and now than in ancient history, and he couldn't tell them very much about Margaret Ross. He did explain about the stone tablet though.

"Aye," he said, checking a tide table that was pinned up on the wall. "'Tis about now ye'd see it. Never in the winter, when there are great wallopin' seas, but just noo a lot o' the clabber's shifted."

"Who *was* Margaret Ross?" Oliver said firmly. "And who was Agnes?"

Duncan stared at him. There was a very prolonged silence. Prill and Colin were watching closely. They couldn't decide if the Scots boy really didn't know very much, or simply wasn't telling.

"Well, come on, you must know *something*. They were *Rosses*." The clipped little voice was beginning to sound impatient.

Duncan laughed awkwardly. "Hark at him. It was years ago, mannie, hunnerts o'years."

"You still must know *something*," Oliver repeated doggedly.

Duncan took a deep breath, and bent over the dismantled shotguns with his oily rag. "They were sisters," he muttered unwillingly. "Agnes was the wee'n. Aye, wicket Aggie Ross. She was burnt for a witch on Carlin's Crag. The auld witch finder got her."

"And Margaret?" whispered Oliver urgently. "What about Margaret?"

"Och, puir mad Margaret, she'd bin awa' wi' the fairies a guid whyle."

"The *what*?" snorted Colin.

"He means she was simple in the head, a bit touched," hissed Oliver.

"What happened to her?" Prill said, in a dead kind of voice.

"Drooned. On the foreland below Lagg's woods."

"Executed," corrected Oliver.

"Murdered. Ye've seen the stane. Why d'ye ask so mony questions?"

"Because of *this*," said Oliver dramatically. "Do you mind moving those up a bit?"

He spread a dark cloth on the table. (It was his best navy T-shirt so he'd have to avoid getting oil on it.) Then he tipped out the contents of a small polythene bag, and bent over them.

"What on earth—" started Prill.

"Hang on, hang on, *wait*," Oliver said irritably, sorting the bones out and referring to a small blue book in his hand. "That goes there... no, *there*, and those are all in a line, and this... goes at the bottom. There. Now you can look."

Duncan, Prill and Colin bent over the T-shirt. The bones were white and scrubbed. Oliver had pinched his mother's bleach and given them a good soaking. Mr Grierson's *Handbook of Human Anatomy* lay open on the T-shirt too, and the three children looked from one to the other in silence. Neatly displayed on the cloth, clean and unbroken, perfect apart from the odd missing piece, was the skeleton of a small human hand.

Prill's stomach turned over and she stepped back. Colin looked more closely and said nothing. Duncan calmly began to fit his father's big shotgun together again. "Where d'ye find 'em?" he asked, quite casually.

"At Lochashiel, in the mud where we moved all the stones." Oliver was talking rapidly and his mind was racing ahead. "If Agnes *was* a witch they couldn't bury her remains in consecrated ground, could they? So they'd cut down what was left and... and just throw it somewhere, over a cliff into deep water, *or*—"

"Or down a well," said Colin. Yes, it certainly made sense.

"Och no, mon," Duncan sounded very scornful. "Ye canna tell that frae a haunful of auld banes."

Prill saw Oliver's face and drew her breath in sharply. He'd stepped away from them all, and was standing on his own in the middle of the dusty cottage floor. A curious stillness had come over him, he seemed bigger somehow, almost threatening. Every muscle in that puny frame was taut and trembling, and his strange pale eyes bulged slightly as he glared at the poor Scots boy with utter disdain.

"It *is* Aggie Ross. It *has* to be. Don't you see? What was left of her was thrown down that well and covered up. They had to make absolutely sure that all that evil was well and truly dealt with, for ever. Now we've come, centuries later, and dug her out again. That's why she's giving Grierson such a bad time, and if we don't put those stones back where they belong it'll go on and on. Surely you understand what's happening, Duncan?"

"Don't talk daft, mon," the boy said uneasily, stirring the fire up with an old poker. He was actually grinning to himself at the thought of Grierson's "bad time". If a witch was abroad at Lagg what did it matter to them? "We're no fashed," he said harshly. "Let him git auld Jockie Ballantyne to the hoos, and hae a wee bit o' prayin' an' sich like. The lassie doesna come roond *here*, ony road."

Oliver could hardly speak. His voice broke as he got his words out, not because of tears but because of the most enormous anger. "You're wrong, *wrong*," he thundered. "You're up against something more powerful than you realize. It's not just Mr Grierson, we're *all* threatened. She could cause a terrible accident, start fires, bring a house down. She might have a go at Alison. Women like that used to murder little children. Use your *brain*, if you've got one."

At the mention of Alison, Colin slipped his hand into Prill's, and gave it a squeeze. It was one of those uncanny moments when they felt strangely awed in the presence of Oliver. He wasn't like anyone else they'd ever met. He saw more than other people, he saw *beyond* things. They knew now, beyond all possible doubt, that everyone at Lagg was in danger from Aggie Ross, and that Oliver was absolutely right.

It was hard to tell what effect his words had had on Duncan. The boy had flushed dark red and was hunched closer to the fire, still poking at it.

Oliver was scooping all his bones together. He put them in the plastic bag and knotted it at the neck, then he rolled his T-shirt up neatly. "I'm going home," he told the others. "It's useless staying here. Are you coming?"

"Your dog havin' pups then?" Duncan shouted out, as they opened the door. He liked the Blakemans, and he didn't want to part on bad terms.

"No," said Colin. "Why?"

"Look at the painch on her. She's swellin'."

Prill bent down and prodded at Jessie's stomach. It was certainly fatter than usual, and curiously hard too. The dog growled softly when she felt the girl's hand, and

165

backed away.

"She's a glutton, this dog," Colin explained in a cheerful voice. He'd noticed the swelling but he didn't want to alarm Prill. She adored Jessie. "It'll be something she's eaten, I expect. She'll be OK."

But Duncan didn't seem to think so. He felt the dog's belly himself and said "I'd get the vet tae her. She's no' weel."

Oliver could have kicked him. He'd been keeping a very close eye on Jessie since she'd eaten the bread, and she'd started swelling almost at once. She seemed in no discomfort but her stomach was getting steadily bigger, like dough rising. A vet would be no use, just as the doctor, called in to look at Colin the other evening, had pronounced him "a fine laddie", and dismissed the headaches. Both would go on suffering, and getting worse, till Agnes Ross was dealt with. But tonight there'd been no point in trying to persuade Duncan to dismantle the dry stone wall and restore the cairn. He'd been so hard and scornful about everything Oliver had said.

He fought with two moods as they picked their way down the spooky back road towards Lagg, frustration at the boy's ignorance about the Ross sisters, and anger at his whole attitude. He and his father were no better than Grierson, really. They seemed equally full of hate and spite, they couldn't forgive. Every time that stake was replaced, or the letters cut afresh into the granite slab,

Hugo Grierson was put on trial yet again for what a long-dead ancestor had performed, centuries ago.

Grierson. That name was on the stone. Grierson the Witch Finder had put Aggie Ross to death on Carlin's Crag, but he'd obviously executed her older sister for witchcraft too, and quite differently. The inscription on the stone was puzzling. "*Within the sea, tyed to a stake! She suffered for Christ Jesus' sake.*" The same man had obviously executed saint and sinner. There must be more to the story of Margaret and Agnes Ross.

CHAPTER NINETEEN

The next day they saw Duncan again. It was raining and they'd gone up into the hayloft to escape from Aunt Phyllis.

"Come on," Oliver had whispered, as they stood finishing the breakfast dishes. "Let's disappear now, or she'll find us something else to do."

But they'd only been sitting in the bales for five minutes when they heard the Rosses down below. Colin peered through the hole where the ladder came up. "It's all right," he mumbled to the others. "It's only Duncan and his father. Mr Grierson's not there."

They all scrambled down to watch the saw mill in operation. Jessie wouldn't stay up in the bales on her own. She'd become very adept at getting herself up and down that rough ladder, but now she had to be carried. She lay like a baby in Colin's arms as he struggled down, listless and glassy-eyed. The swelling on her underside looked much bigger than yesterday. Prill had made her father promise to send for a vet.

"How's yon dog?" Duncan shouted, above the noise of the machinery.

Colin shrugged, and pointed. He couldn't stand this whining noise for very long. He'd woken up with another headache, and it was getting steadily worse. The pills the doctor had left were doing no good at all.

Duncan left his father operating the jagged, four-foot blade, and came over to see for himself, gingerly stepping over a foul, slippery pink mess on the floor. Oliver glanced at it in disgust. He'd stayed behind for a minute when the others were going up the ladder and inspected it. It was the rotting remains of some animal, almost certainly a cat's, the heart and liver were still quite recognizable. Somewhere in the neighbourhood somebody's poor moggy would not creep home tonight.

Oliver wondered what terrible rites involved the skin and fur of a poor animal like this, and whether, if he went back to the crossing in the woods, he'd find Aggie Ross had been there?

He nudged the stinking pile with his foot and uncovered something. While the others were fussing round Jessie he bent down and picked it up gingerly. It looked like a lump of rags but Oliver could see something else in it, a pulpy egg-shaped body with dangling legs and a round head that rolled over to one side. Stuck on top were some disintegrating shreds of rusty-coloured wool, and thrust right through the middle, between the eyes, was a long rusty nail. The boy went cold. Headaches. A mop of curly red hair. *It was meant to be Colin.*

Prill had seen him. There was no time to do anything

but stuff the thing behind some old boxes. Quickly he came over to look at the dog. He wanted to divert his cousins so he showed unusual concern. Oliver hadn't much feeling for animals but Prill cared more about Jessie than she did about most people. He'd heard her crying last night, and Uncle David had promised to get hold of a vet.

Duncan was bent over Jessie, kneading her stomach gently. "She's warse," he muttered. "She's swellin' like a wind-ba'. Get the vet tae her, she'll dee, else."

"The vet's *coming*," said Colin. "Mr Grierson rang him. Don't go on about it, please. My sister's upset."

"*Grierson?*" The Scots boy half laughed, half sneered. "Ye should no' be trustin' *him*. Get the mon yoursel, I'm tellin' ye."

Angus was doggedly operating the mill, feeding wood in. They were making fencing posts. Grierson had had the order on his desk for weeks, and ignored it. Now the customer had been round and made a scene. It was a situation that had obviously put Angus in an even worse mood than usual.

"*Duncan!*" he hollered suddenly, above the screaming of the blade. "Come here will ye, an' gie ower yer bletherin!"

The boy left the dog and crossed the filthy floor. Too quickly. He slipped in the gooey pink mess and went hurtling towards the spinning blade, flinging his hands out wildly to stop himself falling straight on to the machinery. The air was thick with fine yellow dust, the noise was deafening, and the boy seemed quite incapable of slowing himself down. He was hanging over the blade itself, only inches above it, his body swaying to and fro, his terrified freckled face edging nearer and nearer to the murderous spinning disc with its great teeth.

Angus, half lost in clouds of sawdust, had stopped feeding the wood in, but in that second he seemed quite incapable of movement, even though the mains electric switch was just behind him, within arms' reach. He was goggling at his son as he swung over the saw, as if hypnotized, and the three children were staring too, transfixed and helpless. It was as if, in those few seconds, time itself had slowed down and stopped, as if they were all frozen in solid ice and no single person could stretch out a hand to save him.

Duncan knew he was being *pushed* towards that blade. He could feel cold little fingers buried deep in his neck, and above the sickening whine of the machine he heard a thin, high-pitched scream of monstrous laughter as his head was forced further and further down, to be cut to ribbons, if not severed entirely.

He cried out, three strangled words spat like bullets from his lips as the unseen fingers spread themselves in a cold web across his face, killing all resistance. "God help me," the boy was screaming. Consciousness and will were deserting him, he would simply fall forwards limply and that would be the end of it. The saw would cut him to shreds like some big stuffed doll...

Then he felt different hands upon him, and another small, thin voice that he recognized at once, and had never much liked. It was whispering in his ear, urging him back to safety. "Come *on* Duncan," Oliver was saying, standing on tiptoe to try to get his arms round the other boy's shoulders. "It's all right really, come *on*. Come over here, and sit down for a minute."

But Duncan's body was like a lead weight. He seemed deaf to all Oliver's pleading, it was as if his feet were planted in stone, and the cold, bony little fingers were still pushing him and thrusting him, tightening their hold as the thin, hysterical laughter grew louder in his ears.

Then someone else came, nobody they could see or hear. Neither boy ever spoke about it afterwards but both smelt a sweet country smell, new milk, and hay, and the freshness of wet fields, both felt the strong, warm arms wrapped round them, the hands that pulled them firmly back, away from the threatening blade to safety; both heard two voices, the manic laughter that grew more and more animal-like, spitting and screeching and dying away at last to a frustrated growl, the deeper, calmer voice above it, murmuring words of entreaty, and power, and hope.

It had all happened in seconds. Duncan, with Oliver's arm round him, was now staggering blindly about the floor. Angus had switched the saw off at the mains and a shattering quiet had suddenly fallen on the old shed. Oliver found a wooden box and shoved the Scots boy down on to it. Colin, seeing an old brush lying in a corner, grabbed it and tried to swab up the slippery mess that had sent Duncan sliding across the floor in the first place. Prill felt too shaky to do anything but stand and watch, her arm round the trembling dog, her ears tuned to the sound of that awful, screaming laughter as it thinned and died. *She* had been here. Prill knew that, without the boys saying anything.

A violent argument was now developing about Duncan's carelessness, and Angus, out of sheer relief, wouldn't listen to reason. "Ye could ha' lost your *heid*!" he was yelling. "How many times have A tel't ye tae mind the machine, ye daft fuil!" he bellowed, as the Blakemans crept outside into the drizzle, with Oliver.

He was very silent as they walked back. He would never again doubt Prill's romantic fancies. It was exactly as it had been in church, both sisters had been there, the one bent on unimaginable horror and destruction, the other struggling to preserve and help, a strong, silent presence, white magic against black.

Sure enough, very late that night, when he was tucked up in bed reading, he saw a piece of paper being slid under his door. It was from Duncan Ross. "Tomorrow" the big round writing stating simply, "Five a.m., by the field wall."

Oliver set his alarm and shoved it under his bed.

When at last he fell asleep there was a satisfied little grin on his face.

After a day's rain the atmosphere towards evening grew clammy and close, and in the night a terrific dry storm blew up. Nobody slept much because of the heat and thunder. A chimney pot was struck and came crashing down on to the slates, and the grown-ups were scurrying about and talking in loud stage whispers at about three in the morning.

Below Ramshaws a rotten tree tottered and fell, completely blocking the back road. The Rosses didn't hear the crash above the scream and howl of the great wind, and Duncan, having delivered his note to Oliver much earlier, slept soundly, with his father's big shotgun by his bed, cleaned and oiled, and ready for morning.

Behind closed doors, down in Lagg's dungeons, all three children lay awake, listening to the storm. Oliver had shown the other two Duncan's note immediately, and there'd been no argument. After the scene in the saw mill Colin had no more doubts about the presence of Aggie Ross and knew they must carry out Oliver's plan as soon as possible. Prill had never needed any persuading.

Jessie, curled up by her bed, moaned quietly all night. She'd been sneaked in, last thing, from the stone kennel, she seemed so ill. The vet hadn't turned up. Perhaps Duncan was right and Mr Grierson hadn't actually phoned him. Aunt Phyllis, no animal lover, had surprised them by bringing down a dose from Granny MacCann. The animal certainly looked most peculiar now, all blown up like the Michelin Tyre man.

"It's a herbal mixture," she'd said briskly, handing over a small bottle that contained a greenish-yellow liquid. "She says it'll cure anything in dogs. She's got a new cat, by the way. That granddaughter brought it while I was there – that fool of a girl that 'lost' the baby. Anyway, it's just a kitten, but it made itself at home all right. It leapt straight on to Granny's shoulder as if it belonged there."

"*Yes*," Prill thought suspiciously. She still had grave doubts about Granny MacCann. When nobody was looking she threw the "dose" down the sink. Jessie wasn't having *that*, it might kill her.

Colin was already awake and dressed when Oliver tapped on his door. He wouldn't have slept much even if there'd been no storm, his head was aching so badly. He was glad to get up and move around. They collected Prill from her room at the far end of the dank corridor. Oliver slid the kitchen bolts back, and they slipped out into the dim early morning.

Nobody spoke as they tiptoed past the huge outer door of Lagg, turned down the drive and walked through the wet grass, out to the big field where Duncan was already waiting for them. The repaired wall was visible from the house, and they kept looking back, and up to the top floor. All Grierson's curtains were still shut tight.

"We should be grateful for that storm," Oliver whispered. "I mean, bringing the chimney pot down. He's catching up on his beauty sleep, otherwise he might be on the move soon. He always gets up early, according to my mother."

Duncan had already dismantled the new bit of wall. He'd had to climb over the fallen tree to reach the bottom road, then make his way across the fields. Even so, he'd been there just after four and worked for a long time in semi-darkness. Now that he'd decided to go along with Oliver's strange plan he was more anxious than anyone to get on with it.

It was back-breaking labour and it got steadily worse. The two older boys handled the barrow between them, and Prill and Oliver went on ahead, up to Lochashiel. Lagg's woodlands had never seemed more sinister than on that misty August morning. The very path seemed to close in to nothing, as they toiled up the slope, and the heavy trees linked hands over their heads, shutting out light and warmth. Instinctively, Prill took hold of Oliver's hand and held it firmly all the way. Even the pretty stone cottage looked foreboding, and they sat by the well in total silence, waiting for the others to arrive, both knowing She was near, and getting nearer.

As Duncan and Colin struggled up the track with the

barrow the great hare leaped in and out of the shadows, following them like a dog. Colin opened his mouth but Duncan's dark scowl silenced him. "A've seen," he whispered. "Dinna fash yoursel', yet." His gun was up at the cottage, laid ready behind a wall.

The creature hovered near them all the way up to Lochashiel, and back down to the field again. For two weary hours they pushed and loaded and emptied and rebuilt, till their backs were bent double and their hands were sore and bleeding. The heap of stones by the hole in the wall hardly seemed to get any smaller, and the barrow became harder and harder to push up the stony forest path. It was as if the craggy boulders had turned to lead inside it, as if they were ramming the wheel up continuously against some invisible brick wall.

Oliver had brought a mysterious plastic carrier bag with him. All the time he was with Prill, up at Lochashiel, he'd kept it close by his side. What he had to do he wanted to do on his own, so he waited till she'd gone off into the trees with the other two. Then he acted quickly, removing a whole layer of stones himself and scattering his collection of small bleached bones among the lower ones. Next, with a lot of puffing and blowing, he shifted one of the biggest boulders, and underneath it laid the shapeless rag doll he'd found in the saw mill, but not until he'd pulled the long sharp nail out of the sagging head, and flung it away into the bushes.

When it was done he breathed deeply and sat in the

sunshine by the old well, waiting for the others to come back with another load. He would never tell Colin what he'd found in that mess of entrails on the mill floor. He would never tell Prill. That was his secret. It would be sealed up soon, with the remains of Aggie Ross. Let it be buried with her; that was the best way.

At long, long last, the job was finished. The sun was up, and their throats were as dry as paper. They all stood round the cairn of stones in the little garden, thinking of the pure spring water, bubbling away somewhere, deep underground, but also of a small leathery corpse, withered into a shapeless lump by the devouring flames, its head no doubt torn off and set up in the town for all to see, the rest flung unceremoniously down this well, then filled up with stones.

Duncan took his gun at last and levelled it, but with shaking hands. The hare was very near them, sitting back on its fat haunches, its whiskers quivering. In the pale sunlight its sleek fur was like dappled silk. He took aim, but the gun barrel dipped and wavered. "Och, I cann…" he muttered, removing the gun from his shoulder and wiping his forehead. His crushed, frightened voice was addressing Oliver.

He was in control now. They all knew it. "You *must*," said the firm command. "It *must* be killed, Duncan. It's deadly. If it isn't got rid of what you've just done is useless."

"A'll have *nocht* tae do wi' it," the boy said in a trembling voice, and he laid his gun in the grass and went to stand by the garden wall, with his back to them. The hare didn't move.

"It's beautiful," Prill whispered sadly. "Don't you think perhaps—"

"*It must be killed*," repeated Oliver, and he took up the shotgun himself.

His experience of pulling a trigger was limited to shooting tin ducks at fairgrounds, and he usually missed those. The gun was heavy and, as he took aim, he swayed about slightly, his legs almost buckling beneath him.

"Margaret," he whispered in a voice that no one could hear, "Margaret Ross, help us now." And as he stood there a great calm came over him, like light stealing up on you in the very early morning, like unexpected music playing softly, in a lonely place.

All eyes were on Oliver. They saw his finger tighten on the trigger and everyone covered their ears. Prill, a horrible sick feeling suddenly sweeping over her, screwed her eyes up tight. The shot rang out, tearing apart the silence of the dark woodland, sending showers of birds clattering up into the sky. There was one loud scream, the full-throated cry of a woman in the utmost agony of pain. Then silence.

With the smell of the shot still strong in their nostrils they all stepped forwards and looked at the spot where the hare had been. There was no fur, no flesh, no entrails, only a small patch of very dark blood that, even as they watched, shrank away to nothing and disappeared into the peaty ground, leaving no mark.

Duncan bent down and picked something out of the grass, rubbed it on his sleeve then held it out for the others to see. It was the silver bullet, made centuries ago to kill Grierson of Lagg, a bullet of pure Scots silver. "The only thing that would kill a witch." Oliver took a step nearer and saw, before Duncan slipped it into his pocket, that it was whole and unmarked, as perfect as the day it was made.

Now it was really over they all felt jangled inside with a mixture of strange feelings. They were weak-kneed and tearful, and glad, and hungry, all at the same time. So when Duncan had put his gun to rights, and slung it over his shoulder, they set off down the forest path, all keeping very close together. But there was a lightness and a spring in their step that they had not felt for a very long time.

CHAPTER TWENTY

There was no more strange violence up at Lagg Castle. Jessie's peculiar swelling gradually went down, Colin's headaches stopped and Aunt Phyllis made a whole batch of excellent loaves. Oliver grew quite smug. If it hadn't been for him, Aggie Ross would still be at large, shattering the night silence with that terrible lunatic laughter, destroying harmless pets, haunting them in the house and in the woodlands, a mere shadow, a mere breath on the wind, but always there, The Hag, and the fear of her never to be shaken off.

A few days afterwards Prill went to the island with Oliver. Colin had gone off with Duncan Ross, and he had offered to row her across to the castle. He was much slower than Colin, and he splashed a lot, but Prill simply went round in circles and got nowhere. If she'd been able to manage a boat better she'd have come to this place more often, on her own. Although half afraid, she still hoped she might see the figure again, with its little goat on a string.

"She's still around, Oll," she said, as they sat by the loch eating their sandwiches. "I heard her again last night. She's still haunting Lagg, and she sounds so unhappy. What does she *want*? Agnes has gone, thanks to her, but *she's* not at rest, is she?"

As usual he was very thoughtful, and sat with his chin in his hands for a long time before replying. He'd not stopped doing his research into Lagg and its history, but now the violence had ended it all seemed much less urgent.

"I admit that I was wrong about one thing," he said, foraging in his little army rucksack for something else to eat. "Getting rid of Agnes hasn't made any difference to Mr Grierson's behaviour. He's worse, if anything. Somehow I felt if we were to deal with *Her* it'd sort of, well, *humanize* him. It's not, has it?"

"No," Prill replied fiercely. Mr Grierson had gone mad about the hole in the wall. He'd put it down to trespassers, of course, creeping in when the place was quiet, and nicking a load of green stone for something they were building. Stuff like that didn't come cheap. They were all hoping he wouldn't take it into his head to wander up to Lochashiel. He might ask awkward questions if he saw that neat cairn. His latest threat was not to do the promised repair work up at Ramshaws in time for winter, and there were no signs of anyone being organized to come and remove the fallen tree either. It needed heavy machinery, and was far too big a job for Angus and Duncan.

"Why don't they just *go*?" Prill said. "Why stay on, just to be humiliated?"

"They belong here. Angus was born at Lochashiel.

He knows every tree in these woods. He… I don't believe he *could* live anywhere else, now. I think he'd die. Anyway, the Rosses have been here as long as the Griersons. Why should they go?"

There was a silence, then Prill said, "He's very unhappy, isn't he? If you look at him when he's not looking at you, he's not really hard at all. He's, well, sort of *tortured* and guilty-looking, as if he really doesn't know what's happening to him, underneath."

"I know what you mean," Oliver replied. He was thinking about Grierson's diary, of those tortured extracts from the Psalms in their curious red mirror writing, of the man's sense of guilt and rejection, of his loneliness, of his pain. He'd thought it was Aggie Ross, leading him on in all his foul behaviour. There was more to it, though, and Margaret was the key to his agony. Poor mad Margaret whom his devilish ancestor had sent to a terrible death, on that stake in the sea.

Oliver's theory was that Prill's presence had attracted Margaret. He'd been up to Granny MacCann's several times with his mother, and listened while the old woman prattled on.

"Puir mad Margaret," Granny had called her, and she had explained that the figure with the goat was only seen when the "wee'ns" were around. She'd troubled Lagg before, when Helen was a child, and the girl had been sent away to boarding school when she was seven. Only then, according to Granny, did Grierson have relief

183

from the strange, haunting singing, the sorrowful face at the windows, the mouse-like scrabbling at doors and keyholes. Aunt Phyllis took all this to be the wanderings of a very old woman, drawing on confused memories, but it made excellent sense to Oliver. There was a young girl at Lagg again, two, if you counted Alison. So the figure had come back.

"What does she *want*, Oll?" Prill said desperately, when she'd heard all this. "She's begging us to help her, isn't she?"

"The witch finder committed a great and unjust crime against her," Oliver announced dramatically, "and no one in that family has ever put it right. I think what she wants is, well, not *revenge* exactly, but... some kind of *justice*."

The night of August 17th, the anniversary of the drowning, was a terrible one for Prill. After a long day's wooding with Duncan Ross, tracking deer above Carlin's Crag and picnicking up at Lochashiel, the two boys dropped into bed at nine o'clock and slept soundly till next morning. But Prill, who'd lazed all day on a sandy beach, was horribly awake. She heard the ugly grandfather clock in the hall above strike one, then two, and when at last she fell asleep all her dreams were nightmares. If she was dreaming.

It began with great blasts of wind; the bedroom window suddenly burst open and swung to and fro in the gale. Prill waited for the pale, familiar shape to appear in the black gap, for the pathetic tap-tapping. But nobody came. She found herself crossing the room and staring out into the wild night, except that it wasn't night any more but a soft day in late summer, and she was looking along a white sandy path that led straight to the sea.

Now she was being dragged down that path to the familiar moon beach, ropes cutting deep into her wrists, thorny twigs being poked into her eyes and mouth as she cried out; a crowing rabble were all round her, bearing her along in triumphant mockery, and among the faces she recognized the bloated Grierson of Lagg, grinning through his long, tangled beard, and a small gypsy-looking girl, vicious and dark, whom she knew was Agnes Ross.

The narrow path dropped sharply down to the water's edge, silver-white in the midday sun but marked with small black signs of the Cross, where the witch had been. The soles of her feet were tattooed with them so that, wherever she walked, she could tread upon the saviour and his Passion. Prill knew all about witches now, from Oliver, but where was he? And where were her parents, and Colin? She was going to her death and they'd left her alone, and no one was there to put out a hand to save her.

As she stood bound to the great black stake she felt the icy ebb and flow of the tide, and she saw the swirling murderous waters lapping higher and higher. Now they were washing at her shoulders, now at her neck. The faces on the shore were a gibbering pink blur, there was laughter and hysterical screaming.

The tide came at her now, in one huge wave. Her head was covered, water filled her mouth and nostrils, poured in her ears, and she was sick, choking. She began to cough horribly as the wave pulled back, dribbling and vomiting, suffocating on her own bile, and the ropes on her wrists and feet cut into her like knives, while all the time the people that stood watching screeched and yelled, waving their sticks and flapping their flabby white hands.

The wave came again, stronger, higher, lashing at her like a huge cat o' nine tails, beating away at her face, and her poor bruised body, as it slumped down the knobbled black trunk. The shrill dinning of the water in her ears was so loud she felt her ear-drums had split, and were running with blood. There was blood on her tongue, in her eyes, round her lips, and her murderers were crying "Blood, blood," as death came to her, in that dark and bloody sea.

Then, over the din of the crowd, she heard her own voice ring out, steady and firm. "Who shall separate us from the love of Christ? Shall tribulation, or distress, or persecution, or famine, or nakedness, or peril, or sword? As it is written, for Thy sake we are killed all the day long, we are accounted as sheep for the slaughter, Nay, in all these things we are more than conquerors, through Him that loved us..."

At this the goggling spectators jeered and spat, and shouted filthy words, but her voice went on, strengthened, and began to sing—

> *"Let not the errors of my youth*
> *Nor sins remembered be;*
> *In mercy, for Thy goodness' sake,*
> *O Lord, remember me."*

Prill had heard it so many times before, in the deep woods, out on the little loch, here, in her own hard bed. She sat up, wide awake, and the tears ran down her face, but as the voice in her head grew more pleading, more insistent, the full horror of Margaret Ross's terrible death washed over her, like the bitter tide itself, and she began to scream uncontrollably.

Four doors away, Aunt Phyllis turned over in bed, opened her eyes, and listened. The girl really did sound as if she was in excruciating pain. Prill's door was pushed open and her aunt, still half asleep, stood over her, peering curiously into her eyes. Had she been sleep walking?

"No, no, *no*!" screamed Prill, pushing violently at the woman's face and dislodging her hairnet. At that moment, the thin, disapproving mouth and small hard eyes were those of all the wicked tormentors Margaret

Ross had ever known.

Oliver's mother prided herself on her tact. She came away from the bed muttering something about "late suppers" and "overstimulation", shut the window firmly, got Prill a hot drink and a water bottle, and sat patiently by her side till the girl's eyelids began to droop at last. It was certainly cold down here at night, and perhaps a bit creepy too, for a child. She must have had a nightmare.

"Forget it now, dear," she whispered, as Prill drifted off. "Whatever it was, forget it. We're going to that sale tomorrow, remember. Perhaps we can find something pretty for you, a souvenir of the holiday."

Who on earth wanted to remember a holiday like *this*? Even as she fought against the heavy waves of sleep Prill felt thoroughly indignant.

They all went to the sale. Aunt Phyllis held them all up by insisting on changing into her best at the very last minute, and when they arrived the bidding had started.

It was in a huge country house a few miles down the coast. An eccentric old woman had lived alone in it for years; now she was dead and the house had been bought by some local builders, for conversion into luxury flats. This was the sale of the effects.

Everyone they knew was there; the Rosses, Granny MacCann and troops of her relations, the two women that cleaned up at Lagg, the man who'd mended all the windows, even Mr Grierson, looking in disgust at the litter of sandwiches and beer cans at the feet of the prattling MacCann tribe. The sale was just an excuse for a trip out, to them; they'd not even bought a catalogue between them.

Grierson had, and he'd come for just one thing. It was a rather poor oil painting put into a job lot with several empty gilt frames and two cracked mirrors. It was old, but the artist had been a dabbler, not a painter. He reckoned he'd get it for twenty or thirty pounds.

The Blakemans had to stand right through the auction; people moved about all the time, looking at things, but as soon as a seat was emptied somebody filled it up again. It was a bit like musical chairs. All sorts of fascinating bric a brac went under the hammer. Aunt Phyllis got some pretty custard glasses, Dad bought a teapot for Mum, and Angus Ross secured a polished brass shell case to stand by his fire. But Oliver had eyes only for one thing and as soon as Grierson moved away from Lot 48 to talk to somebody, he pulled the others over.

"*Look*," he whispered. "*That's* what he's here for. I bet you anything."

Colin and Prill followed his finger. The painting hadn't even got a frame and it was almost falling to pieces down the cracks. It had obviously been folded up and kept flat in a chest of drawers or a cupboard for a very long time. It was a double portrait, of two girls.

One was thin and dark, with a reddish skin and masses of long black hair. It was a pinched, nasty little face with something strangely twisted about the mouth. The eyes, black as ripe sloes, looked straight at you, hard and unsmiling. On the narrow forehead was the distinct mark of a cross. The girl at her side was larger, and not so dark. She was paler skinned, with soft, curling brown hair. It was a sweet and generous face with a large mole on the left cheek. She was looking, not at the artist, but downwards, at a small creature cradled in her bare, plump arms, half hidden under a plaid. It was a baby goat.

The border of the painting was curiously elaborate, an endless wreath of leaves and berries, and tiny animals. Oliver thrust his face close up, to inspect the details, but Prill couldn't take her eyes off the two faces. There they were, together at last, Agnes Ross and her sister Margaret.

Hugo Grierson didn't get the picture. A small bespectacled old man in a pepper and salt country suit seemed absolutely determined to have it, and the bidding went up and up. Mr Grierson's face was a dark, angry red, his fingers, white and rigid, were clenched round the knob of his carved walking cane. Amid mounting excitement from the crowd, the price rose higher and higher. It went at last for a hundred and twenty pounds, to the other man.

As the hammer fell Grierson snorted and pushed his

way out, and a spotty-faced youth with a notebook immediately rushed up to the buyer and started to bombard him with questions.

"*Galloway News*, Dr Gillespie," they heard, and "Now just what *is* it exactly, about this item? Could you give me a few details?"

There was no further opportunity to examine the picture. Dr Gillespie sat guarding it for the rest of the bidding, and the minute the sale finished he was on to the desk with his cheque book, the tattered canvas tucked firmly under his arm.

"So that's that," muttered Prill, desperately disappointed. "We'll never see it again now. I actually wish old Grierson had got it. It belongs to Lagg anyway."

But three days later Oliver slipped off secretly, in his usual fashion, and walked the three miles into Kirkmichael for the *Galloway News*. He was hours coming back, and Prill and Colin sat waiting for him, in an agony of frustration, when they realized where he'd gone. One look at his face told them it was in.

"Come on, come *on*," hissed Colin, as Oliver sat down at the kitchen table, carefully unfolding the paper and smoothing it out. The more serious the matter in hand the slower and more deliberate he became. He could be maddening sometimes. Together with the "Grand Flounder Trampling Contest" at Palnackie, the auction had made the middle-page features.

"There you are," he said, jabbing a finger and sliding the paper across the table. He looked calm, but his voice was high and squeaky with excitement.

The heading ran "*Intriguing Discovery at Country Sale. New Light on Local History.*" After setting the scene, the spotty reporter had written:

"*The painting was eventually bought for an unusually high price by local historian Dr John Gillespie of Kirkcudbright who believes it to be a portrait of the tragic Ross Sisters of Lochbean. Agnes, the younger girl, was known to be in the pay of the infamous Grierson of Lagg, the 'witch finder' of notorious local repute. Through her lies and machinations the pious, simple-minded Margaret was condemned as a witch and executed on the beach below Lagg Castle, by being 'tied to a stake till the flood o'erwhelmed her', drowning, in those days, being considered a 'kind' death for a woman.*

"*Far from dabbling in witchcraft, Margaret, though apparently weak-minded, was a devout Christian, and stoutly refused to admit that she had ever consorted with The Devil. As the floods rose, and she was urged to confess by her agonized parents watching on the shore, she is said to have cried out, 'I will not. I am one of Christ's children, let me go'. Contemporary accounts state that she sang hymns as the waters rose up around her, and that she calmly quoted from the book of Romans – 'Who shall separate us from the love of Christ? Shall tribulation, or distress, or persecution, or famine, or nakedness, or peril, or sword?'*

"*Dr Gillespie points out the large mole on her cheek which, at her trial, was said to be a 'witch mark'. It is known too that the unfortunate girl had a passionate feeling for all animals, including goats, which she tended for her father. The goat, of course, is the animal most closely associated with Satan. She was well-practised, too, in the art of herbal cures, and this also was raised at her trial as evidence of witchcraft.*

"*Her sister Agnes's real motivation for exposing this harmless creature is lost in history, but some thirty years later she herself was tried as a witch, again by Grierson, and, along with two others, was burned at the stake above Carlin's Crag. It was proved at the trial that the three had been responsible for the deaths of several new-born children in the neighbourhood, had celebrated the Black Mass, and had committed many other atrocities against local people, 'there beasts and there lands'.*

"*Dr Gillespie points out the intricate border to the portrait, the berries of the 'magic' rowan tree being interwoven with pictures of a leaping hare. In country lore the hare was a shape often assumed by a witch. The mark on Agnes's forehead is blurred but it is almost certainly a cross. In Scotland, proven witches were branded in this way, before being led to their deaths. The absence of any such mark on Margaret's face is intriguing.*

"*He concludes that the painting is poorly executed,*

and indeed, highly fanciful. Nevertheless, the unknown artist was clearly possessed of much information about the Ross Sisters, may well have witnessed both executions, and done the portrait soon after the death of Agnes, c. 1715. An expert on Scottish witchcraft, Dr Gillespie regards the death of Margaret Ross as 'one of the saddest martyrdoms in history'."

"Why did she do it?" whispered Prill in a broken voice. "Why did she let her own sister be put to death, when none of it was true?"

"Because she was a witch," Oliver replied slowly. "A *real* witch." He was thinking of those jokes about poor old Granny MacCann, who was nothing more than a harmless, eccentric old woman. "Because she was wicked. There *are* wicked people," he added quite simply. "And she was one of them."

CHAPTER TWENTY-ONE

A few days later the three children stood in a line in front of Hugo Grierson. After a lot of argument, and more than one change of heart, they'd decided to beard the lion in his den. The portrait was finished, and they were going home in a couple of days, but not before they'd tried to get something done for the Rosses. Nobody else would speak up for those two.

Colin was the official spokesman. As he listened to the carefully-prepared speech, Oliver quaked inwardly. If she'd known where he was, his mother would kill him, but they'd chosen their moment with care. A weekend trip to Edinburgh had been planned to round off the holiday, and Mr Blakeman had gone to collect a hired car in Kirkmichael. Aunt Phyllis was with him, shopping for little souvenirs for her old people.

Their attempts to persuade Mr Grierson were doomed from the beginning. Colin started quietly enough, saying how they'd noticed that Ramshaws leaked, and how Angus said the roof wouldn't last another winter, then Oliver chipped in and suggested that the Rosses could be moved to Lochashiel. Prill, misinterpreting Grierson's silence, was encouraged to suggest that the saw mill might have a bit of cash spent on it too. "The blade's exposed you see," she explained, in her sweetest, most reasonable voice, "and there could be an *awful* accident."

Grierson's silence was not the silence of a man listening to sense, and being persuaded. It was speechless outrage at the enormity of the situation. That the three of them should dare to sneak upstairs, demand access to his private rooms, and stand here telling him what to do... three *children*.

"Get out!" he said suddenly, in a tight, hard voice. He wasn't shouting, but he'd flung the door wide open and he was pointing at the stairs. "Get out this minute, and we'll say no more about it. But if I were your father," he went on, looking straight at Colin, "I'd beat the living daylights out of you, and I hope he does!"

Prill and Oliver lost their nerve when they saw the sheer malice in Grierson's face, and scuttled to the top of the back stairs. But Colin stood his ground. In fact he got his foot in the closing door, and was forcing it open again.

"Listen," he said through clenched teeth, now losing his head entirely. "You hate them, don't you? You just *hate* them. You know they won't go, so you – you make their life absolutely unbearable. What's the point of it all? We only came up because we're going home soon, and we like them, and... and because you make everything so *miserable* for them."

Grierson took two steps forward and delivered a

stinging slap across Colin's face. The pain brought tears to the boy's eyes, and there was blood seeping through his teeth.

"*Go!*" the man screamed. "Get down those stairs before I throw you down, and break your neck. That's what I'd *like* to do. And tell your father what the hell you like. I don't care."

"I'm not a sneak," Colin spluttered, half sobbing with pain, "and I'm not a bully either." But Grierson had already slammed the door and was standing by his desk, still quivering with rage and staring blindly down at the stake on the wide, empty beach, a single dark spear thrust up from the pale sand, like the accusing finger of God.

He was still there, looking down, when Colin came out of the trees and began to walk out towards the sea. He was hurt and humiliated, and he wanted to be on his own. He wanted to come here, where Margaret Ross had suffered and died. There were wars in the world all the time, fighting between people who couldn't trust one another, between people who couldn't forget the past. That was the trouble with Grierson and the Rosses, they nursed old wounds, wounds that should have healed long ago.

Forgive and forget. He could just hear Aunt Phyllis saying it now, when he and Oliver argued over something. How much poor Margaret had to forgive, sent to that unspeakable death by her own sister.

"Help them," Colin said aloud, staring far out over the shimmering sea. "Help them all." But the harsh cry of the gulls drowned his own wavering voice, sounding like human cries.

A fire broke out in Lagg's woodland the night the Blakemans were in Edinburgh. Grierson was alone. None of the staff slept in any more, apart from the housekeeper, and Aunt Phyllis had gone off with the Blakemans – he'd insisted. His nerves were so jangled by those outrageous children he wanted the house to himself for a couple of days. No, food wasn't a problem, he didn't want any food. Just drink, thought Aunt Phyllis, her lips thinning to nothing. She'd seen Grierson tipsy on more than one occasion. Angus Ross drank too much as well, down the The Thistle in Kirkmichael. Two of a kind those men were.

Duncan was asleep at Ramshaws, and he was quite alone. His father always went drinking on a Saturday night and sometimes came home early on the Sunday morning. He'd taken the dog with him. Mac would have barked at the first wisp of smoke to come under the door, but he wasn't there to give a warning. He'd been lying patiently in the snug at The Thistle, at Angus's feet, hoping someone might throw him a scrap or two.

Something woke Hugo Grierson just after one o'clock. The windows were open and there was an unfamiliar smell in the room. He was out of bed in seconds, the thick drapes were dragged back, and he was staring across to Carlin's Crag. It was moonlight, with a thin scattering of stars, but the smooth white face of the great rock was wreathed in a shifting grey cloud, darkening at the edges to dull scarlet.

For a second the man went rigid, then he turned, grabbed the field glasses he always kept near his bed, and focused them on the dark spread of trees that fell from the sky down to the wide lawns and borders of the garden like a massive stage curtain. His woods were on fire, and the heart of it was above Carlin's Crag. But there was a cross wind blowing, and, even as he watched, a ripple of flame waved across the Crag towards the seashore, lighting the tops of a row of pines like the fuse on a giant firework.

Grierson groaned inwardly. He'd been lucky, there'd not been a major fire at Lagg for years, but what rain they'd had recently had been fitful and short-lived, hardly enough to dampen the ground. The woods were tinder-dry and, with the prevailing wind, conditions were ripe for a real blaze.

He wasn't prepared. Like everything else in recent years, emergency measures for fighting big forest fires were dust-covered in his mind, and there was nobody within miles; even the campers had packed up their neat tents and gone home... there were phone numbers though, and procedures he must follow. For the odd, isolated flare-up, Angus Ross always got a few cronies together and they combed the woods with beaters, great witches' brooms the man had made himself, for thrashing the flames out. But this was already too far gone for a few locals.

Feverishly, Grierson dialled emergency. The voice at the other end was sympathetic but unhelpful. Yes, they'd got all the details and Yes, they would come, but the whole force was already out – Forestry land was ablaze near Dalbeattie. Whatever Grierson could do with his own estate workers he should do. They'd get to him as soon as humanly possible.

Estate workers. The man's mouth twisted as he slammed the phone down. There were no such men at Lagg Castle any more. He knew his woodlands were neglected and unproductive, that thousands of pounds needed spending on them. All he'd got was Angus Ross and a handful of yobs who helped him during the summer, and he hated Angus Ross and his works to hell…

Minutes later he was driving up the back road to Ramshaws in the Range Rover. The stony track curved round through the trees. They were still untouched but smoke was already drifting across the windscreen, and even through closed windows he could hear the muffled crackle and spit of the flame. He couldn't stay here very long.

He rounded a steep bend and screeched to a sudden and shuddering halt. His way was completely blocked by something black and enormous lying across the path. Grierson got out and looked, cursing himself for not getting the haulage people in to remove the fallen tree. Angus Ross had asked several times, but he'd brushed him off. "It can wait," he'd said. "You don't take your van up to the cottage anyway. Let it wait, man. Money's tight. I've not got it to burn."

Now it was all burning, years of slow silent growth, tiny limp seedlings planted by his grandfather, that had weathered frost and snow and wind, strengthening to springy young saplings, towering up into magnificent trees. In their prime the jaws of the fire were devouring them, a life-time's planting swallowed up in smoke.

He looked helplessly beyond the fallen trunk, the arm of a monstrous giant flung out, blocking his way. Now and then, as the grey gusts waved and billowed above the flames, he could see the ramshackle roof of Ramshaws lit by bright moonlight.

Grierson went cold. The boy was in there, and he was alone. He knew Angus Ross's drinking habits. After a long night at The Thistle the man'd be flat out on someone's grubby sofa, down in the town, sleeping it off. The smoke was thickening and the fallen tree had now caught at one end. If Grierson climbed over it to try and reach the cottage he may well be choked, and pass out before he was halfway there. They'd find him afterwards, like a shrunken charred log lying on the path, another victim of the fires on Carlin's Crag that had burned three witches, centuries ago.

The path behind was still clear. Grierson got back into the Range Rover and reversed crazily down the track, leaving it slewed in the middle of the empty space at the bottom where Ross always parked his ramshackle old van. Like a man in a dream, light-headed, and curiously detached from his own body, one foot moving mechanically in front of the other, Grierson walked back along the bottom road, turned in at a gateway, and followed a narrow track that led across to the bottom of Carlin's Crag.

The night was quiet here, apart from the steady crackle of flame. His ears were pricked but there was no sound, yet, of anything making its way towards him. He could go back to Lagg and dial Emergency again, but what was the use? The boy was asleep and alone in Ramshaw Cottage. By the time they got up to him he'd be dead.

Let him die, a thin voice whispered inside him. Duncan Ross, fourteen years old, a fighter like his father. *Let him die*, the son that Grierson had never had, the grandson he'd never even seen. *Let him die*, this boy who was bound to his father Angus with cords as strong and deep as whatever bound Ross to the great forest itself. With the boy dead, the man would surely leave Lagg for ever. It would be as good as killing him.

Grierson looked up at the Crag. Ramshaws was directly behind it, tucked away in the shelter of a small overhang of rock that served as a natural wall. Above it, and on each side, the woods were blazing but the glaring white knob of stone had contained the downward spread of the flames. MacCanns' and Lochashiel were not threatened, yet. Carlin's Crag rose up above him, smooth and untouched by the straying fingers of fire.

It was the only way. The man struggled over the barbed wire and began to climb, slowly at first but speeding up as he got higher. Halfway up a tiny ledge jutted out, hardly visible from the ground but just wide enough for his feet. He gained it, leaned against the cold rock, and panted, hardly knowing how he, a sixty-year-old man, out of condition through drink and lack of exercise, had got himself so far. Yet he'd climbed with all the spring and lightness of a seventeen-year-old youth in the prime of life, his hands and feet hardly needing to feel their way up. It was as if someone strong and confident was guiding him to safety, every inch of the way.

Grierson put his burning cheek against the cool of the Crag, and breathed deeply. He needed to calm down before making the last part of the ascent. There were no footholds left, they'd been worn away years ago. It was a death-trap for climbers. He closed his eyes, and the spiteful little voice inside him dried up to a harmless whisper, and was lost in the crackling trees. Another voice was in his ears now, and another face was before him, the calm forgiving face of Margaret Ross, the grave, sweet face of the old portrait, the voice steady and kind. It was she who had helped him this far, and seconds later he'd started to move upward again, crawling spider-like up the unclimbable Carlin's Crag, in a strength that was not his own.

In less than five minutes he was at Ramshaws, trying to get the door open. The boy was slumped behind it, unconscious, and Grierson kicked and hammered at the rotting timber. Panic was clawing at him. The flames were all around the old cottage, the roof was ablaze, and the heat was soon pushing him back towards the Crag. His eyes streamed and his lungs were choked with bitter smoke. But he'd got the boy, lying in his arms like a bundle of old rags.

Grierson stumbled back blindly, the way he'd come, all strength gone. At last he stood motionless above the glaring white rock that looked, from below, like a ghostly white face framed in wild grey hair. Noises came to him on the wind, above the hiss of the flames, men shouting and the howling of sirens. Peering down, he made out flashing lights, and men scurrying like ants up and down the moonlit ribbon of road, looking for water.

He didn't know if Duncan Ross was alive or dead, but his feet remained embedded in the rock. There he would stay till someone came; he wasn't going to let him go.

And people arrived quite soon, sooner than he'd dared hope. Black-coated men, curiously masked, looming towards him out of the smoke with ropes and blankets and a small flask which they shoved roughly between his lips, telling him to drink.

But there was no arguing with Grierson, even now. The boy was moaning and shifting in his arms, but the man kept a tight hold of him and he went between two firemen, stumbling and falling about, being guided along, close to the edge of the rock where the fire had no hold. There was no track at all but they picked their way expertly down, through the smouldering trees, the woods behind blazing like one gigantic bonfire, with all the witches there had ever been, and all their wickedness, heaped up for kindling.

At last he was walking across towards the road, still clutching Duncan to his breast like a tiny child, across a small paddock towards a little knot of onlookers waiting by one of the engines, while firemen tore about with pumps and hoses.

He remained conscious just long enough to hand the blanketed bundle over to Angus Ross who stood alone by the roadside hedge, hollow-eyed and haggard, with tears running down his face. Then he swayed gently, and fell forward in a faint, hitting his head on the road before anyone could catch him.

CHAPTER TWENTY-TWO

The Blakemans had planned to go home after the Edinburgh trip, but in the end they stayed on. Grierson actually asked them to, through his doctor. He had not cracked his skull, despite his heavy fall on the road, but the shock of the forest fire, and his climb up the Crag, had obviously proved too much for him. He was resting in bed, and had to be kept very quiet. They thought he might have had a slight heart attack.

Oliver, trotting up and down the back stairs with trays of food provided by Aunt Phyllis, was quite shocked when he saw him. He seemed so much older and very shrunken-looking, propped up in his great bed with its view across the gardens to Carlin's Crag. His skin was papery-white and his voice was a whisper. He actually said thank you, when Oliver brought the trays up.

His plight didn't move Colin much. It'd take more than a minor heart attack to change his views about Grierson, in spite of his heroic climb. They couldn't agree about why he'd saved Duncan Ross, or how, in practical terms, he'd got himself up the Crag at all. "I bet he thought twice about it," Colin said savagely. "Pity he didn't fall off. The firemen would have got to Duncan anyway. I'm glad he's OK."

"Don't be so foul," Prill replied coldly. "What a cruel thing to say, wishing he'd fallen off. You're as bad as he is."

Oliver said nothing at all, but he knew that Colin was probably very near the truth. He could so easily have left Duncan Ross to die. As it was, he'd brought him and his father home to Lagg, given them a couple of bedrooms, and got the doctor to check that Duncan hadn't suffered in any way from those hours in the smoke-filled hut. The fire had been put out before it reached the lower cottages and a builder had been sent to have a look over Lochashiel. The roof needed patching up and there was a bit of damp, but apart from that, and the need for a good spring cleaning, it was ready for the Rosses whenever they wanted to move in. Ramshaws, which they'd always hated, was now a blackened ruin.

Helen Ross came to Lagg the minute she heard about the fire, and her father's illness, and she brought Jamie with her. It was a tense day for the Blakemans. She didn't go up to the tower rooms immediately, because Grierson was asleep, but sat in the kitchen eating Aunt Phyllis's ginger cake, gossiping about Lagg and its neighbourhood, and cracking jokes with the children.

"Can't believe *she's* anything to do with Grierson," Colin said a bit later, watching her with Jamie and Alison, under the great oak. "I mean, she's so… *normal*."

Helen was very young-looking and arrived wearing

pink dungarees and a rainbow-striped sweater. "He's such an old misery," she whispered to Mr Blakeman, "I decided he needed cheering up. He's always rather enjoyed wallowing in the glooms." Helen could walk on her hands right round the oak tree. "The only useful thing I learned at my horrible boarding school," she yelled to Oliver, from upside down. Oliver tried it, but fell flat on his face. He couldn't get the knack at all.

Aunt Phyllis wasn't too sure that she approved of this garishly-dressed young woman. Her mental picture of Grierson's daughter had been quite, quite different, and did this person actually realize what a difficult man he was? They'd not met for more than four years, after all. She waited knowingly for Helen to come straight down again from Grierson's rooms, for the shouting to start, for Helen to fling her suitcases into her funny old car, strap Jamie in, and go. But Helen did not come down.

She stayed with her father for more than two hours and all Aunt Phyllis could hear were low voices talking together on the other side of the door. Glancing up at the tower suite from the garden, Oliver could just make out the shape of Helen and her father standing side by side, watching Jamie swinging madly to and fro, in the great oak.

Prill didn't meet Helen till the first evening. She'd slipped away to Hag's Folly, determined to get to the island on her own this time. She was glad Colin wasn't around, to laugh at her efforts with the boat. It took her a long time to get across in the little blue dinghy, but she managed in the end, and tied it up firmly in the shadow of the crumbling tower, below the patch of grass where she'd once seen the goat.

Margaret had gone, she knew that the minute she stepped on to the shingle. This had been her place of sanctuary, and it was here she'd been apprehended by Grierson's men, and taken away for her trial. Oliver had found this out. He'd discovered too why that cellar floor was all concreted over. The island had been rented out all one summer, to some Americans, but they hadn't stayed; they'd been frightened by the strange noises that came from under the castle, by an unearthly voice that sang to them at dead of night, and by something that stood in that cellar doorway, silently watching them.

Had the cellar led down, perhaps, to the ancient tunnel under the loch? The tunnel that came up on the grey-green slopes of the Hill of Doon? The tunnel where the poor lost piper had starved and died? And was Margaret hiding there, when the witch finders came to hunt her down?

Prill felt sad when she thought of Grierson, pathetically ordering concrete to cover a floor, thinking that that alone would be sufficient to seal up a chapter of a bloody and terrible history. It had done nothing to silence poor Margaret then, though she was silent now.

The girl wandered about, unable to get into the boat

and row away. There was no nibbling goat, no familiar country smell, no quiet presence, no voice singing above the gentle lapping of the water. "Not revenge but justice," Oliver had said, and justice had been done now. Not "a life for a life", but a young life preserved, by someone three hundred years beyond death. Duncan's life, a life that could easily have been lost if Grierson, in that moment of time, had not stopped hating, had not made his miraculous climb up Carlin's Crag to save him, and so undone the hate and hurt of centuries.

The minute Helen Ross came back into the kitchen, Aunt Phyllis bundled Oliver off with a tray, and shut the door. She wanted to find out exactly what had happened up there, and it wasn't a conversation for children's ears. "*Now*," she was saying, as he made his way up the cold back stairs, "what about some more tea for everybody? And, er, how did you get on, Helen?"

"I left him writing his diary," came the answer, cheerful but evasive. "Yes, I'd *love* some more tea."

There was no answer to Oliver's knock, so, balancing his tray precariously on one arm, he pressed down the great brass handle and went in. Grierson was propped up in bed against a mound of pillows, but his eyes were closed, and he was snoring gently.

The boy realized that this may well be the last time he'd ever be in this room. What a bit of luck that Grierson was asleep! He put the tray on the bedside table, taking great care not to rattle the china together, and began to creep about. In the library there was still a strong smell of putty, and also signs that Grierson had been clearing up. A lot of pictures had been taken down, for example, among them the old wool-work sampler with its curious text, "*Thou shalt not suffer a witch to live.*" It was tied up with string, together with some badly-stained prints of animals and birds. Oliver smiled a little smile. Odd that Agnes Ross hadn't singled that sampler out, when she wrecked the library. The text must have been the gospel of the man who'd sent her to her death, that black-beard on the stairs, old Grierson of Lagg.

The red leather diary was open on the desk. The entry was short, but very heavily ruled off, as if this was the last time Grierson would ever write in it. "*Have been talking to Helen about schools for Jamie,*" Oliver read, "*No chance of her sending him away, so no grandson at the old Academy. Pity. The boy's obviously destined to be a Caithness crofter, like his father. Still, he seems a cheerful little chap.*" Then in red, waveringly, as if, in writing, the man had fought hard with some deep and terrible emotion, there was another of those quotations from the Bible. It was not familiar to Oliver but he knew it couldn't be from those agonized Psalms. It was just two lines, and the boy read them over and over again. "*And the harvest of righteousness is sown in peace by those who make peace.*"

There was nothing more.

If the man was going to sleep all evening he may as well take the tray down again, but when he crept through into the bedroom Oliver had a slight shock. The big mahogany bed was empty and Grierson, in a dark silk dressing gown, was standing by his window, looking out on to the ravaged hillside. He turned round when he heard the light footsteps.

"I just came for the tray," Oliver stammered, realizing what a close shave he'd had. "I didn't want to disturb you so I—"

"Looks awful doesn't it?" Grierson cut in, quite lost in a world of his own. "You can't put trees back in five minutes, you know."

"Will you plant some more?" the boy asked nervously. He surely wouldn't. The man was a miser, and it'd cost thousands of pounds. Angus Ross had said so.

"Oh yes, I'll replant," Grierson said quietly, "And it'll be beautiful again in time, you'll see. Yes, I'm going to replant."

Because it was a time for planting, for putting rich soil round withered old roots, and it was a time for sowing good seed, where nothing good had ever grown before.

Witches have been hunted down and killed over many centuries, though at certain times in history this became particularly intense, and both Church and State employed official witch finders. In 1486 the *Malleus Maleficarum* (Hammer of Witches) was published. It was written by two inquisitors and was long regarded as the leading authority on all matters concerning witchcraft.

In Britain, the persecution of suspects reached its height in the seventeenth century. James I had written his famous work on demonology in 1597, and took a personal and somewhat bloodthirsty interest in the hunting down and torturing of those found guilty. Biblical references to the subject (above all *Exodus* 22 v. 18, "Thou shalt not suffer a witch to live") were interpreted with fanatical zeal. Though, undoubtedly, some indulged in the foul practices described in this book, many thousands were quite innocent, the victims of mass hysteria, or of an individual's lust for blood. One such fanatic was the historical Grierson of Lagg.

A girl might be proved a witch if she had moles or warts on her body, such things being "the Devil's mark". An eccentric old woman, innocently dispensing herbal cures, might be dragged out and executed, as might anyone suffering from epilepsy, schizophrenia, or other mental disorders. When the persecutions were at their height, such abnormal behaviour was inevitably pronounced to be the work of Satan.

Most famous of all witch finders was Matthew Hopkins, who emerged in the 1640s as the champion Witch Finder General of the Eastern English counties. He was hated and feared, but eventually perished when his own method of swimming a witch was tried upon him, and he drowned. This ordeal involved tying the suspect hand and foot and throwing her into deep water. If she floated it meant the water had rejected her, proving her guilt. If innocent, she sank. Attempts (not always successful) would then be made to rescue her. Witches were not burned in England, but in Scotland many thousands went to the Fire, often after being subjected to the most hideous tortures.

The historical Margaret Wilson ("puir mad Margaret" of this story) was not, in fact, executed for witchcraft, but for refusing to obey the laws forced on her by the Church. With her younger brother and sister she left home and joined the rebel Covenanters, zealous Christians who would not accept rule by Bishops, but who chose to worship in their own way, in secrecy, and against the law. Many were hunted down and killed. Thomas and Agnes Wilson escaped punishment but the eighteen-year-old Margaret stood firm.

After prolonged imprisonment, and a ludicrous trial at which no evidence for the defence was allowed, she and the aged Margaret McLachlan were pronounced guilty, and were sentenced to be "tied to palisades fixed in the sand, within the flood mark of the sea, and there to stand till the flood overflowed and drowned them".

The sentence was carried out at Wigtown on 11th May, 1685. The old woman died quickly. Her stake had been driven in further out on the sands so that the sight might inspire the young girl to recant. It made no difference. She met her own end with immense bravery, singing Psalms and quoting a majestic passage of courage and hope from the Book of Romans. When asked to recant she said, quietly and deliberately, "I will not, I am one of Christ's children. Let me go."

Her memorial stone, listing the names of her persecutors, among them Grierson of Lagg, may still be seen in Wigtown churchyard. Her death is regarded by many as one of the most tragic martyrdoms in Scottish History.

A.P.

COLLINS MODERN CLASSICS

Black Harvest

by

Ann Pilling

The rugged west coast of Ireland seems like the perfect place for a holiday. The only snag for Colin and Prill is that they have to go with their weedy cousin, Oliver.

But their brilliant holiday never happens. It's stiflingly hot, and there's a really foul smell around – a smell of death of decay. Prill starts to have terrifying dreams, and baby Alison becomes desperately ill.

Colin and Prill are hot, sick and confused. It is only Oliver who looks as if he knows what is going on. But even he doesn't know everything…

Collins*Children'sBooks*

Visit the book lover's website
www.fireandwater.com

The Beggar's Curse

Ann Pilling

When Colin, Prill and Oliver arrive to stay in the village of Stang, they soon realise that there's something terribly wrong with the place.

Prill feels something sinister in the ancient rituals of the village play. Colin knows the 'accidents' that keep happening are something much more gruesome. Only Oliver seems to know the truth. He understands the dark secret the village is hiding and senses that it comes from the black waters of Blake's Pit. He can even feel the terrible power of *the beggar's curse...*

0 00 710270 4
£3.99

www.**fire**and**water**.com
Visit the book lover's website

The Empty Frame

Ann Pilling

When Sam, Floss and Magnus are sent to stay with Cousin M at Bisham Abbey, they do not expect that it will be very exciting. Then, on the first night, Magnus is woken by the sound of sobbing and finds that the portrait of Lady Alice Neville has become an empty frame. Gradually, the children are drawn into a 400-year-old mystery.

Who was Lady Alice and what is her terrible secret?

0 00 675293 4
£4.99

Order Form

To order direct from the publishers, just make a list of the titles you want and fill in the form below:

Name ....

Address ....

....

....

Send to: Dept 6, HarperCollins Publishers Ltd, Westerhill Road, Bishopbriggs, Glasgow G64 2QT.

Please enclose a cheque or postal order to the value of the cover price, plus:

UK & BFPO: Add £1.00 for the first book, and 25p per copy for each additional book ordered.

Overseas and Eire: Add £2.95 service charge. Books will be sent by surface mail but quotes for airmail despatch will be given on request.

A 24-hour telephone ordering service is available to holders of Visa, MasterCard, Amex or Switch cards on 0141- 772 2281.

Collins
An *Imprint* of HarperCollins*Publishers*